ABERDEEN
CITY LIBRARIES

www.aberdeencity.gov.uk/Library
Tel: 08456 080937 or 01506 420526

Cults Library
Return to........Tel: 01224 868346..................
or any other Aberdeen City Library

Please return/renew this item by the last date shown
Items may also be renewed by phone or online

08 MAR 2016
09 May 2017
? 09 June 2017

Also by Frances Fyfield

Helen West series
A Question of Guilt
Trial by Fire
Deep Sleep
Shadow Play
A Clear Conscience
Without Consent

Sarah Fortune series
Shadows on the Mirror
Perfectly Pure and Good
Staring at the Light
Looking Down
Safer Than Houses

Diana Porteous series
Gold Digger
Casting the First Stone

Other fiction
The Playroom
Half Light
Let's Dance
Blind Date
Undercurrents
The Nature of the Beast
Seeking Sanctuary
The Art of Drowning
Blood From Stone
Cold to the Touch

A PAINTED SMILE

FRANCES FYFIELD

SPHERE

First published in Great Britain in 2015 by Sphere

1 3 5 7 9 10 8 6 4 2

A CIP catalogue record for this book
is available from the British Library.

Hardback ISBN 978-0-7515-5519-6
Trade Paperback ISBN 978-0-7515-5520-2

Typeset in Plantin by M Rules
Printed and bound in Great Britain by
Clays Ltd, St Ives plc

Papers used by Sphere are from well-managed forests
and other responsible sources.

MIX
Paper from
responsible sources
FSC
www.fsc.org FSC® C104740

Sphere
An imprint of
Little, Brown Book Group
Carmelite House
50 Victoria Embankment
London EC4Y 0DZ

An Hachette UK Company
www.hachette.co.uk

www.littlebrown.co.uk

To Julian Machin,
Creator, Curator, Obituarist,
Playwright and Inspiration.

And also to Grace.
With love and thanks.

ACKNOWLEDGEMENTS

Thanks to Henriettea Boex, Glyn Winchester and all at the Falmouth Art Gallery, who staged an exhibition called A Question of Guilt in April 2015. The success of this was because the life-enhancing gallery in Falmouth is as different as it possibly could be from the fictional institution described in these pages.

I've borrowed a little from the geography of the Falmouth Gallery, for which, apologies. Otherwise, no resemblance (rather a reverse image), and many happy memories.

Thanks also to Barbie, Jennifer Davies, Prosper Devas, Eileen Gunn, Liz Mott and my sister Susan Styan, for seeing me through.

PROLOGUE

Opening picture. *A young woman with hair the colour of sand sits with two companions round the fire. Waiting for a storm.*

Diana Porteous could see this room as a portrait of her life. A large, high-ceilinged room of graceful proportions facing the sea in a big house that was formerly a school. The walls were covered with vibrant oil paintings of different subjects and interiors.

The room was both a study and a gallery, giving it an atmosphere of learning and, at this moment, just a little bit of ennui. The email Diana Porteous was showing her two friends had arrived the week before on an evening when Di had been looking out to sea. The view from the windows often distracted from the pictures on the walls. This evening, it was moonlight on calm water, a sublime work of art in itself. Di handed a printout of the email to Sarah and Saul.

'Letter from a distressed curator,' she said.

'So it is,' said Sarah. 'Do you get many of these? How exciting.'

Dear Mrs Porteous,

I'm the curator here. Only the part-time curator. I'm holding my breath and writing you a letter instead of screaming.

In response to your enquiry, dear MS Porteous, I don't know the answer! You were looking for a particular painting by that woman, Eve Disher, which we are supposed to have. Somewhere.

I'm not supposed to be writing back to you, but the Director ignored the request. We have some wonderful oil paintings in our stores, all listed, photographed and then put back. Not digitalised, oh no, and the records are a bit . . . We probably have the painting you mention, acquired circa 1956. Fact of the matter, we have a lot of paintings down in the store, several by very good English artists. Problem is our new Director doesn't like them. Doesn't like oil paint, full stop.

Painting is nada. Instead, there's a video installation in the major space, and a model cow the size of a house with six legs and two tails, all created by an Outreach project last year. The video installation features a mouth opening and closing. Apart from that, the walls are empty, although there are luminous footprints on the floor, leading you from one space to the next in case you can't follow. Even the school parties are bored. The only things they like are our life-sized mechanical toys, manufactured locally at a time when automata and such things were fashionable. They were used as advertisements outside shops, thus a metal waitress would sit outside a café, and if you put a penny in a slot, she would raise her teacup and put it down again. There's a dog that will wag its tail for tuppence. Ghastly, garish animated dummies, and of course the Director adores such kitsch, probably because they're obedient.

Fact of the matter, I might be able to find the painting you're seeking, but in the mess of the middle floor downstairs, it might take a week or three. What's there doesn't correspond to what's supposed to be there, or to the catalogue I did when they were last on show. He just stacked them up, rather artfully, to make room. Got to innovate, he said. Make space work. And so he stops me finding anything.

Sorry, sorry, sorry, Mrs P. I'm not making sense.
But he keeps rearranging everything, and when I
notice he interrupts me. Still, I've been looking for
the painting you want to see, and what has upset me
so much is the fact that there could be an awful lot
missing. When I realised that, I was horrified, and
then I thought, perhaps it's better if they have been
stolen. Perhaps we need more thieves in this
museum. At least if the paintings are stolen, they
have a chance to see the light of day. Better be
stolen than rot in the dark, I say.

Someone is coming to look over my shoulder.

My dear Mrs P, it might be easier if you just
came and looked for the painting yourself. Take it
away if you can find it.

Sorry.

Winifred Doris, Curator

'It's an invitation to burglary,' Sarah said joyfully. 'Let's
do it!'

'It looks like she was writing this late in the evening after
a drink or two and a bad day at work,' Saul said. 'What on
earth did you suggest to her to set her off like this?'

'I sent a letter to her Director, asking to see a painting
I know they have. I said I had a great portrait by an artist
called Eve Disher on my wall, and I'd love to see more of
her work. Research via a website told me they had one in

4

their collection, not on display, like so many aren't. I asked could I have an image of it, or could I come and see it? That was the reply. I was trying to track down other works by artists we already have. You know how it is. Part of ongoing research. Part of being a collector, seeing what else the artist did.'

'Have you ever been to this Kemsdown place?' Sarah asked. 'It isn't far.'

'No,' Di said. 'I didn't know of it.'

'An invitation to steal,' Sarah repeated. 'What an excellent idea. We need something like that.'

'Oh, stop it, you two,' Saul Blythe said. 'I thought we were having a preliminary discussion about our proposed forthcoming exhibition, the first in our wonderful new space. Let Me Remind You,' he said, speaking in capital letters, 'that we're trying to compile an exhibition of sorts. We are *not* currently collecting or researching; we are preparing for our first interactive exhibition. With a theme as yet to be determined. We must make a selection, and then link it to a theme. Concentrate. One thing at a time.'

'So we are,' Di said, stretching and yawning. 'Summit conference coming up tomorrow evening. Patrick's working on it. We need the input of a child and he wants to announce the theme. Enough for now. It's drawing classes for both of you and Patrick and Peg all day tomorrow. Saul, you're modelling for the painting classes, with

Patrick. Sarah, you're doing the Life Drawing class with Peg in the afternoon. And I shall take time off until we have a meeting about the exhibition in the evening. Forget Winifred Doris and her paranoid letter. For now. Although she haunts me.'

'What a shame,' Sarah said, wistfully. 'It's not very often you get an opening like this.'

Saul squinted at the email. 'Good of you to share this with us,' he drawled. 'I think the woman's merely mad and disgruntled in her provincial museum. I'm guessing you've also shared it with your supposed brother, dear Steven?'

'Yes.'

'Must you?'

'Yes.'

Saul left it at that, with a hint of disapproval in the air. He began to think ahead to the next day with real excitement, because that guy would be there at the class. The man called Toby, the real artist, the old man who could really draw and paint, he was going to be there. Di was not going to elaborate on her reply to his question. She smiled at him. They all smiled at one another, acknowledging the fact that they did not tell each other everything. And that nothing was quite as cosy as it seemed.

'Time for beauty sleep,' Sarah said, patting her brother on the shoulder. 'See you tomorrow.'

A day among collectors and would-be thieves: Di, owner of the house and the collection, Saul, collector and agent, both of them made a little morally ambiguous by a passion for paintings; Sarah, with her practical amorality; Patrick, aged twelve and Peg, nineteen, the only innocents of the household, asleep upstairs. And Patrick's parents, Gayle and Edward, full of venom, safely lingering as ghosts in far away London, like snakes in hiding.

Two hours away from their coastal town, Steven Cockerel sat in his eyrie, looking out over Pall Mall with a very different view. He had read the letter from Winifred Doris, forwarded to him by Diana Porteous. He pictured her, sitting in that glorious room by the sea amidst the pictures on the walls, and the image made him content. She could be looking at the picture he had once stolen from her, and then returned, and he would see her soon. Hair the colour of sand, Di had. His half-sister, perhaps.

The view from Steven's windows was over rooftops and down to rumbling traffic, and he wished for it to be the sea. He had been born by the sea and he was a collector, at first of paintings featuring the sea, now of anything. Also sculpture. Paintings had become his passion in the thirty-sixth year of his money-making life, lifting him into moments of happiness he had never otherwise known. The walls of his apartment were not full enough, but every painting represented a moment of triumph, a source of joy and achievement like no other. Paintings made him happy: it followed that acquiring more of them would increase his happiness and therefore his humanity. He wanted more. He wanted the insight and the joy. He wanted to protect; he wanted what no one else had. He wanted the hidden and the forgotten.

He looked again at the letter from Winifred Doris. Did it really amount to an invitation to steal from a public collection? He shook his head. Stealing was wrong, wasn't it? Di had taught him that. You never truly owned what you had stolen; it was never yours. But here, in this letter, there was the suggestion of an opportunity for acquisition. If the Director of this museum despised his stock, perhaps he would be willing to engineer a sale. There would be legalities and restrictions, of course, but there were always ways round that. Steven should know. He was a master of buying at the back door. He was a buyer and seller.

'What do you think?' he said to the statue. 'An idea to be investigated?'

He was speaking to a small, graceful neoclassical sculpture he had recently acquired. John Bacon, about 1690, which made this young woman very old. She wore Greek costume and seemed to be stepping across a river on sweet, sandalled feet. Her left arm, the one which might have been carrying a basket, was missing; she had probably adorned a grave before her abandonment into a rubbish heap. The missing arm was poignant. Steven touched her gentle head and bade her goodnight.

Once he had wanted perfection. Now he loved the flaws. Once he had been an investor into art. Now he was a collector, prepared to negotiate because he was in love.

She was not safe from envy and he wished she was.

Someone was waiting for her to fall.

PART ONE

CHAPTER ONE

Artist. Dictionary definition.

Early meaning: A person who is master of a practical science or pursuit; alchemist, professor of occult sciences, chemist, etc. A person who cultivates or practises one of the fine arts, especially painting.

The wise and the fool. The artist and the unread.

There were many cultural initiatives in this small seaside town where Di and the collection dwelt. The painting and drawing classes were one example. They were held weekly in a room in the old theatre that had been left by a philanthropist to the citizens a hundred years before. A touch decrepit, but thriving due to innovative management and multipurpose use although not always quite warm enough.

A whole day of Art every Wednesday. The morning, for three hours including coffee break, was devoted to head and shoulders portraiture – pen, pencil, oil, acrylic, watercolour, or any medium. Some of the obliging models for this session took the opportunity to wear elaborate costume, including hats. Others dressed for warmth. Two models in the morning for Portraiture, two in the afternoon for Life Drawing. The heat was turned up to emphasise the contrast. Only the students remained dressed in the afternoon; models, no clothes at all. Not a stitch.

Materials required for Life Drawing: paper, pen, pencil only. No paint.

Sarah Fortune was a natural at standing in the nude in the afternoon, because she simply did not care. She had done it often enough and volunteering the other two – young Peg, Di's accidental housekeeper, for the Life class in the p.m., and her brother Saul for Portraiture in the morning, alongside twelve-year-old Patrick – was her idea, based on the assumption that they might enjoy it as much as she did. For Sarah, it was thinking time, in which her mind could roam, frivolous and free. Those drawing her from life concentrated avidly, while she, their model, remained impassive. They shone their bright eyes on her like a series of headlamps, while she thought of everything and nothing and contemplated the joys of burglary.

She was not quite indifferent, on account of being generous by temperament. She wanted to help and she had nothing to hide, didn't mind that her outline was not as sharp as it had been once. There were plenty of remnants of the misspent youth she had not treasured at the time and she had always been best described as handsome, rather than pretty. Relieved to be rid of youth's burdens, especially the guilt. She was what she was, a lissom, forty-five-year old figure, capable of twists and turns, adopting any pose required and able to keep it; flexible in body and attitude. There was precious little that Sarah Fortune had not done before and she found the elderly audience appreciative and kind. She might have modelled for London art schools, but never underestimated provincial students.

Unlike her brother, Saul Blythe, Art Agent and unapologetic snob, who had, at first, no time for the output of amateurs, even though he enjoyed adopting a pose and did it all the time, especially for the morning Portraiture class. Sarah knew these students could have enormous talent, while that was something that Saul, acquisitive Art Connoisseur, had only just begun to learn.

Sarah was indifferent to her creases. How wonderful, not to care. Beauty in its own right; a body come into its own and owned by its mistress, showing the promise that it would only grow older disgracefully and continue to worship the sun. She gave of herself, made eye contact, smiled, willed them to do their best, encouraged them to observe. I'm all yours, she said and listened to their conversation.

Peg was another matter. At twenty years of age, Peg was completely unconscious of her own statuesque curves and was fixated on her own fat. She had a magnificent figure which she hated because she was unaware of anything but flaws. In late nineteenth-century Paris, she would have gone down a storm for a body with shape and style and skin like silk, but for all that, she did not know what she was, so that when she posed for the first time, despite rehearsal with Sarah, she slouched in her nakedness, feeling like shit, glaring at them and wanting to yell, *What the fuck do you think you're looking at?*

She was thankful, now, that she had not actually opened her mouth the first time around. This time, the second time, she gazed at the walls in awkward anger which slowly began to melt. So she had hated it, first time, but still, she had volunteered to do it again. Go figure. They were all quite sweet, really, these geeky old punters, once you started to see their grey hair. So grateful and appreciative and anyway, Peg was such a sucker for the elderly it could be said she was actively in pursuit of a grandparent. And she had to do it, didn't she? Because if she had said no, Patrick might not do his bit either.

It has been suggested, Diana Porteous wrote in her diary, *that models are exploited. Many were, I suppose, but not as many as those who got something out of it. Sarah thought it might be a good way of acquainting Peg with the power of her own beauty. Strange thing is that having done it once, when she almost yelled at them, she volunteered to do it again.*

Forty pounds helps.

Peg is, in a manner of speaking, our housekeeper and more than that. She may keep the skull of my deceased husband's first wife somewhere about her person; another story, never mind. Know what? These classes have gone on for two generations and I never knew even though I was born in this town. Me? I'm thirty years old, rich widow of this parish since two years ago, and Peg feels like a daughter, even though there are only ten years between us. I wouldn't have known about the Life Drawing class when I was a kid on the other side of the tracks. Sarah's an incomer and she did. Sarah's the one who said they needed models. My contribution is to pay for them and get my ersatz family to volunteer.

Sarah first, and then her brother, Saul Blythe, my late husband's agent and now mine, was persuaded to sit for the portrait session, along with Patrick, my late and much mourned husband's grandson. Uncle Jones could not be persuaded, but he will collect Patrick and take him fishing during the Life class in the afternoon. And I get a free day.

I love all these people, but I may love paintings more. I am not in the room, I have gone away, so please take notes and pay attention at the back.

*

The man at the far end of the front row in the first class was a man of talent. The same man could sketch a portrait in oils, entirely at home with his brush. In the afternoon class, he drew like a dream. He got the outlines. He got Peg. He got bolshie Peg with her curves and magnificence, subjected her to the greatest, benign examination, and it was because of him showing her what he had done, last week, that she agreed to do it again. So polite and shy. Old Toby made a day of it, never flagging, although God knows he was pretty ancient and had a tremor. He looked like a man who had painted all of his long life, and canny Saul, dealer by instinct, found his fingers twitching and his hackles rising. Saul was a hunter. The week before, in the morning class, old Toby had done a fantastic oil sketch of young Patrick, one of the best oil sketches of a child Saul had ever seen. No exaggeration, really, really, even allowing for the fact that Patrick was a good model with a wonderful quality of stillness. It was good for talented Patrick to pose for this sweet class of students in a safe place; only for the Portraiture class, of course, fully clothed, alongside Saul in the morning. Part of his education. Patrick had been sketching portraits since he was four and he should understand what it was like to be drawn himself, experience what it was like to be observed while being ignored.

After that, Uncle Jones would take him fishing, just like last week. Saul did not pay any attention to Patrick, forgot his existence. He joined the afternoon class purely for the purpose of watching the man Toby at work, waiting to make his acquaintance. And then he would talk to him, get him to show his other work. *What have you got at home, Toby? You must have wonderful stuff at home, artist like you.*

The oil sketch Toby had done of Saul himself last week was also terrific, although so shockingly revealing that Saul wanted it back. He would offer to buy it from him, he would use his charm, he thought as he skulked at the back, observing closely, waiting to pounce.

Three thirty in the afternoon.

So, Di said to herself, they are all fine. Uncle Jones is on the pier with Patrick. Saul, having done his stint in costume for the earlier class, will be at home, looking at stuff on a screen and guarding the collection while marshalling stuff for our discussion on the proposed exhibition, due this evening when Patrick is going to give us his ideas. Patrick's ideas are vital. Peg is modelling, mentored by Sarah, and me, myself? Owner of a fine house and a collection of paintings which imprison me, I'm halfway up a steep path, freeing my mind and at the same time, wondering about them. My family, not related by blood, but mine all the same. My responsibility, like all the paintings I own and want to share.

Who are my allies? Don't count them.

What am I good at? Don't look.

Who are my enemies? Don't see them, but I must not forget who they are.

And last of all, where am I?

She was on the cliffs, labouring uphill, three miles from home, having left her bike at the foot of the slope, aiming for the lighthouse from where she might be able to see the world. Another uneven half-mile to go, and it wasn't the steep incline that bothered her; it was the fact that she was blind. The low, piercing, late-winter, early-spring sun hit her eyes like a blade of light shining straight at her. Arrows of cold air hit her eyeballs and she could not blink them away. The sun was sinking over the horizon, fiercer than fire. Those coming in the other direction, with the sun behind them, could see, while she could not and she was looking forward to turning back, although that was not an option until she got to the top of the hill for the best view of the sea. She had a momentary fellow feeling with her husband, who had loved this cruel light, although it made his old eyes stream with tears. Thomas, sweet Thomas, with his glorious blue eyes and brown skin.

She knew the terrain so well, she knew she was near the summit, even though she could not see forward and kept her eyes on the ground, conscious of the odd person coming towards her on their way back, deviating to the side and murmuring the customary *Good afternoon.* The view at the top was awesome and there'd be a cup of tea at the caff.

Then someone stopped in front of her, and said hello.

'Hello, Di Quigly, fancy seeing you here. You little thief.'

She couldn't see him. She couldn't even look round him. All she had was the almost-spring sun in her eyes, and the edge of the cliff, close by, twenty yards away and she never walked closer than that. 'Sorry,' she said, 'can't see you. The sun. My name is Diana Porteous, by the way. Not Quigly.'

'Good,' he said, 'I can see you fine. Why are you crying? Come with me. I need to talk to you, I'll lead you up.' The voice was muffled.

She shrugged off his arm and he persisted. 'Look at the view,' he said and he wasn't leading her up the hill, he was leading her sideways: she could feel that. Leading her sideways down the slope towards the edge of the cliff with his arm in hers. She felt she was stronger than him but all the same, helpless. The dog at her heels began to snarl and growl and prance around and at the same time her phone rang. She heard the man curse as he stumbled against her so heavily she lost her balance and fell. Someone yelled, *Stoppit*, and the dog was barking and herself falling and rolling away towards the edge, clutching at chalky earth. Then she was lying in the grass, next to a windblown scrub and a bench, getting her phone out of her pocket and the daft dog was standing guard, barking in a big, deep voice, all shout without bite. Breathless. A matter of seconds. The sea boomed. No one there.

There had been two people there, one pushing, one shouting from a distance.

Patrick, beloved step-grandson, was on the phone, shrieking.

'He's not moving, that one over there, he's not moving at all. Toby, the man in the class. Where are you?'

Di sat up. She was still some way from the edge.

'What?'

'The old guy. The one who could paint. Not moving.'

'Go home, Patrick. I'll be back soon. Where's Peg?'

'She's here. Outside. Class has stopped.'

'Go home, both of you. He'll be fine.'

'OK.'

Di got to her feet and staggered downhill. The dog that should have been dead ambled after her, unfazed. Even the dog could not manage without her. It must be good to be a dog and have such a selective memory.

Go home. The landscape was deserted.

Toby Hanks was dead. Best student in class, Saul's real artist. Dead as a dodo. Even after revival was attempted out the back, the best performer in both the Portraiture and Life Drawing class expired. He was taken to hospital in the ambulance for further attempts to start his heart, but the reality was that he was dead. Better not to believe it.

Peg, in the meantime, had taken twelve-year-old Patrick home to the house by the sea, Patrick asking, 'Why did that man in the front row stop moving?' And Peg saying, 'Probably drunk is why. Fell asleep, didn't he? He'll be alright, don't worry. He looked at me nicely. I fancy fish and chips. What were you doing there, anyway? You'd no business being there. You did your modelling stint this morning. You were definitely not supposed to come back. Why did you? You were supposed to be fishing with Jones, not hanging round.'

Peg was unhappy and she was scolding him, being a nag.

Patrick stopped and shouted, '*Don't!*' You could shout when you walked by the sea because of all the other noises like the waves. You could say exactly what you meant.

'Why did I sneak back? 'Cause I wanted to see the girls with no clothes on, didn't I? I came back and *watched*, didn't I? Jones didn't notice, he was fishing. I wanted to see women without anything on – when else do I get the chance? So did Saul,' he added defensively. 'He snuck in the other side to see what old man Toby was doing. Maybe that's why he stopped breathing.'

'He'll be alright,' Peg repeated. Patrick let himself believe her, although he didn't. They both calmed down.

'And,' Patrick said, 'I wanted to see *you* without any clothes on. *You*, in particular.'

Peg stopped, shocked beyond words, speaking without thinking.

'You wanted to see *me*? Silly, fat me? And what did you think?'

'Don't know why you bother with clothes at all,' Patrick said crossly, as if it was obvious. 'You're fantastic, you are. Everybody's going to want to paint you. You're beautiful.'

'Yeah, yeah, yeah. Silly git.'

They were holding hands, brother and sister. She punched him on the shoulder and he pretended to reel, punched her back. After a bit of sparring and growling, they continued to stagger home, exchanging insults and discussing supper.

'Silly git.'

'Stupid woman.'

'I'm beautiful,' Peg sang out. 'I'm as beautiful as a painting on the wall.'

'Nah, better than that.'

Sarah Fortune, life model and best placed to observe, had been the first to notice how old Toby got up and sat against the wall at the back. First his movements, then his rasping, then his flopping. She had raised the alarm, helped move Toby into the back room, attempted revival before the ambulance arrived and the paramedics made further attempts before taking him away. She had been calm and controlled although shaking beneath her raincoat. Half an hour later, she was being useful, stacking chairs with her brother Saul. Everyone else had gone home.

'All done?' she said.

'Not yet.'

In the dead man's satchel were sketchbooks and crumpled drawings. His oil sketch of Patrick from the morning was still propped against the wall where he had joined it. Shining and wet, a true likeness of a bright and curious face. His sketch of Saul, from last week, was not there.

'I'll take that,' Sarah said. 'I'll pin it up in the back room to dry.'

'And I'll carry the rest,' Saul said, shaken if not stirred. His reaction to this sudden death was dispassionate: it was shocking until old Toby was moved out of sight and everyone carried on, and since then, Saul had gone into overdrive, thinking of the implications. He had managed to find Toby's coat first, removing the keys and address book from the pocket before helpfully handing the man's wallet to a paramedic. He had managed to make all this seem like the actions of a concerned citizen while it was only another sleight of hand. Saul never did anything without a purpose. It was easy to volunteer to look after an old man's things. Old Toby's satchel smelt of paint and turps; the coat smelled of tobacco. Nobody wanted either in a sterile ambulance.

'What are you going to do with his things, brother

mine?' Sarah asked him, wishing she did not know him so well.

'Oh. Take them home for the poor old soul,' Saul said with deceptive carelessness. 'Least I can do.'

And have a good look round, Sarah thought. *You are going to let yourself into the home of a recently deceased man, to see if there are any paintings worth having*. Nothing mattered to Saul except paintings of quality, nothing at all. It was his life and his obsession. Human beings always took second place.

She knew how his mind worked, if not why. How odd it was to love someone so much and yet disapprove of them at the same time.

'Does he live alone?' Saul asked.

'I believe he does.'

Typical of Sarah that she would have unearthed many a detail of the lives of the students, either by asking or observing. People rushed to give information to Sarah; they queued in the intervals to confide because she listened. She could have guessed the man lived alone, though, because of the way he looked.

'Useful,' Saul murmured, giving her his best, innocent smile. 'Are you going back to the homestead straight away?'

'Yes, Di's on her way.'

'See you later, then. Patrick's revealing the theme of our exhibition. I may be late.'

It was still light when they turned out on the street, and Sarah made her way down to the sea. Saul went in another direction, as she knew he would. Her brother had a conscience, of sorts. It just wasn't like anyone else's. She was not his controller.

Let him be. There were things to do at Di's home. The old schoolhouse by the sea was not Sarah Fortune's home, although she was there so often it felt like it. Nor were her brother's passions hers. Sarah had come into the household at Saul's behest to befriend Di in her grief and they were now indeed real friends. She cared for Di profoundly and felt extremely protective of her. The nature of her role as the mature friend was something she often considered, because sometimes it seemed as though Di was the oldest. She had to keep Di distracted from loss, keep her mind occupied, get her out of the house, add some surface sophistication, make her able to don a disguise and use her different talents. Make her more reckless, as they had been before. She must also keep the peace with Saul: create calm; she was good at that. Sarah could also raise hell if need be. She wanted to be a good influence, and also a bad one.

She would help organise this exhibition to open out the collection and put it on the map; she must help Di achieve that and take a place in the wider world. Protect her, for sure – Di was essentially alone and susceptible – but protect her from whom? Predatory men, for a start, of whom

Steven Cockerel with his claim of kinship was possibly one.

The jury was out on Steven, particularly since it was clear that Di was intensely fond of him. And you had to be wary of a man whose flat you had burgled.

In the meantime, on with the show.

CHAPTER TWO

Di had let herself in the back door of her house. It had become a tradition to use the back door. It was sheltered and led into the immediate comfort of kitchen and snug, with access from there into the huge, warm cellar, while the front door faced on to a vestibule and the main, grand staircase. The front door no longer stuck as it had, the old rain-swollen door now replicated with a facsimile of itself, only stronger and artfully double-glazed, shutting and opening sweetly. Peg liked it for slinking in late at night.

Di avoided the front door because it had so many associations. Through this front door, the police had arrived more than once on various fool's errands: once to arrest Di, and another time, to take Peg. And they had come to collect Thomas via that route on the day he had died. So much for all that.

The dog padded around, snuffling at her feet. She was called Grace, on account of having a head like Grace Jones; the size of her enormous head on her thin body seemed to disorientate her. Grace was younger than she looked and was, Di hoped, untraumatised by past experience. She could make her throaty bark for no reason and ate entirely without discrimination. She did not have a jot of spatial awareness, was always in the way and loved everyone almost without reservation. She seemed to have forgotten any cruel treatment she had ever received. Her artless affection had even persuaded Peg into liking her, although that had taken some time.

Fact was, Di remembered being told that Grace had once belonged to old Toby, the man who had died that afternoon in the Life Drawing class. Old Toby had gone into hospital and Grace had been left roaming free, mad, distressed and starving. It seemed as if Toby had forgotten he had ever owned her and had never asked to have her back. Maybe not his fault; maybe he had genuinely forgotten or assumed his dog had found another home; maybe someone had told him so, or told him she was dead. Try as Di might to be forgiving, and forgiveness, both given and received, was one of her specialities, none of this endeared Di to this Toby man she had never met. Saul said he could paint and being an artist justified anything, but he hadn't done good by his dog and she had never known he was an artist. *Let's face it*, she told herself, *you're cross with them all.* Cross with that Toby for dying, not because of the fact of it, but because of Patrick being there and looking at naked bodies when he was supposed to be out on the pier fishing. Cross with Jones for not taking care of him; cross with Saul for not paying attention, cross with Peg. Cross with responsibility. Cross about being pushed on the cliff path, because in her heart of hearts, she thought she knew who it was and she was trying to pretend she did not know. She was trying to keep a lid on that can of worms.

Of all human qualities, she rated kindness highest, was afflicted by it, and did not always feel it. Like now. Felt no kindness towards dead Toby. He was a man who had abandoned his dog through no fault of his own, and who went on to die in the art class, exposing Patrick to trauma. She should feel sorry, but there wasn't time.

There was no one home yet. Di thanked her lucky stars for Sarah, keeping her informed, taking over if need be. Sarah who knew how people ticked and who did not give a fig about art but accepted the nature of those obsessed by it. Di wanted to tell Sarah about the man on the cliff who had pushed her. About the sensation of falling over, blinded by the sun; how she now realised that she had not, at any point, felt severely threatened; no fear that this clumsy attack would have carried on, even without the intervention of the dog or the ringing of her phone. It could have been one of her childhood friends, one of the gang with whom she had been sent out burgling houses when she was twelve and so small she could be stuffed through a crack in a window she had broken. The gang who sent her in via the steel shutters of the now revamped cellar here in this house, with instructions to steal car keys, all those years ago.

She thought of it often, how it was that instead of following those instructions, she had gone upstairs and been magicked by the paintings on the wall, and the sight of Thomas at his desk and had her epiphany in the sudden realisation that what she was doing was wrong. Guttersnipe finds conscience; goes to prison; becomes gold digger/wife of old man; ends up owning large house. That would be enough to make someone angry enough to shove her towards the edge of a cliff. Her ten-year relationship with Thomas, the man she was sent to rob, and who took her in when she came out of prison, was full of love and respect, the best thing that could ever have happened to her in an otherwise lousy little life; she could not regret a minute. For what he was, for the kindness thing, for seeing her clearly, delighting in her, educating her without condescension, making her value her own judgements and all the rest. Di went down to the basement. It had all begun there, in the cellar.

Thomas's ex-wife had drowned in the basement on the

night that Di had come to burgle. Another story that had turned into unspoken legend.

And then Edward and Gayle had come back to steal, embarked on an orgy of destruction and violence. Di shuddered.

Enough. The basement, first purpose-built as an impressive wine cellar, had been underused for the last decade and more. Now, under Saul's care, the place had been transformed, so that it had gone from being two rooms with an artificial partition between the two, back to its former glory of a single place with uninterrupted, mellow brickwork soaring high into two vaulted roofs, lit from above. This was where Saul had always wanted the collection to have its first exhibition, because of its elegant proportions and the huge advantage of having its own separate entrance. *This*, he said, *is where we introduce the populace to the wonders of our world while keeping them out of the rest of the house.*

Di did not love the downstairs; nor did she particularly enjoy exhibitions below ground level, however artful the lighting and however good the reasons for the preservation of pigment. Di liked the upstairs rooms of galleries, where the light poured in, like the huge spaces of the Courtauld with the great windows facing the river. Light filtered by blinds but still daylight. She had seen so many paintings in below-ground rooms with dark painted walls during the course of this last year's travels. Over the months she had been to more galleries and museums than she could count, both to view and pursue ideas. Di knew how to collect paintings, not how to exhibit them. And now it was clear that Thomas's collection had to be exhibited in order to be shared. She had also been trying to teach her perhaps-brother Steven how to look at paintings without thinking of profit. Steven; she smiled at the thought of Steven, looking forward to seeing him soon.

'I'll tell you a secret, shall?' Di said to the dog. 'Steven is not my brother. I know he's not my blood brother. But it's best for now that he believes he is and that everyone else does too.'

Grace agreed.

It was not a relationship of which Saul approved, while Sarah was neutral. Saul thought Steven was a taker, out for whatever he could get. Di thought otherwise. Soon, in London, they would resume their endless conversation and Di had stopped resisting the urge to discuss everything with him.

She wandered through the rooms, as she often did, saying hello to favourite portraits, asking them how they were. Would they like more light, or less? Would they prefer another room? Saul said she would adjust their hats, if she could, dust them down so they could go out into the world and be admired. Di would have liked their first exhibition to be shown in the finest room in the house, once two class-rooms and a study, with the fine old interconnecting doors thrown open to make it one. There, there were wooden floors and huge windows facing the sea. *That would be too distracting*, Saul said, *and besides, you live in that room, it's yours. It's the engine room of this house and this collection.*

So, the basement it would be, although Di was aware of her own, multi-layered reservations. That decision made and the exhibition space almost ready, the next decision to be made was which paintings this exhibition should contain. There were four hundred from which to choose for an initial exhibition, which made it, Saul said, three hundred and fifty too many. Fifty paintings, then, linked by a theme. Which paintings and what theme was something they had planned to discuss this evening, to take advantage of young Patrick's presence among them. They needed Patrick's advice. He knew every painting in the house and they needed the eyes and the ideas of someone who was still a child because it was the young who Thomas had wanted to draw in. *Don't let Patrick be distracted by Toby's death*, she thought, then, *What a heartless bitch I am.*

And am I being treacherous for thinking that I would prefer the first exhibition of the Porteous paintings to be somewhere else entirely?

'Don't think Patrick was too much affected,' Sarah said, lounging in the kitchen, as insouciant clothed as she was naked. 'Peg told him old Toby was going to be alright, and Patrick chose to believe her. After that, I think he was more worried about being in trouble for sneaking into the Life Drawing class to look at women with no clothes on. Little blighter got more than he bargained for. They'll be back soon, right as rain. Peg's in charge. And he's full of ideas about this bloody exhibition.'

'His phoning was a bit timely, by the way,' Di said. 'A man shoved me over when I was walking near the edge of the cliff and then my phone went and Grace growled. Should your insight into my life give you any idea who it might have been I'd be glad to know. I couldn't see, I was blinded by the light and I think his voice was muffled by a scarf.'

Sarah smoked a cigarillo as elegantly as she did everything, put her feet up on the kitchen table and stretched. Old boots protruded from a full skirt of many colours. She was very painterly, Di thought, how Thomas would have loved her. Even her feet looked interesting.

'Were you scared?'

'Not, really, really scared, no. He was so clumsy. I fell, though.'

'Not your dad? Not anyone you could smell?'

'I thought it might be one of my old mates, trying to attract my attention. I just wanted it to be anyone other than my father, because I've been thinking of him. Been thinking I might have misjudged him.'

'But no real fear?'

'No.'

'Not the kind of fear which freezes you?'

'No.'

'Then forget about it. And don't think you're envied in the town. Divided opinions, yes, but a load of sympathy, too. Woman of mystery, but not hated. Give yourself a break. So, we'll put that on the back burner, shall we? Got something else to tell you. Don't know for sure, but I reckon Brother Saul has gone round to Toby the painter's house. I know how he thinks. He reckons there might be some decent paintings. I'm not sure I wanted you to know that.'

Any more than she would have wanted to know that Di had a deep and dark suspicion of who it was who had pushed her on the cliff. She suddenly remembered the smell of him. It was Patrick's father, Edward, with his horrible aftershave smell that had lingered here for a year. She could not tell Sarah that, not now. There was a clatter of voices and steps as Peg and Patrick came in through the front door and thundered down the corridor. Together they were as noisy as starlings: separately they could be quiet and from the heavier footsteps, Di could guess that they had collected Uncle Jones. He would be expecting to be in trouble, too, for being more interested in fishing on the pier than the care of his afternoon charge. Jones could overdose on guilt. Sometimes Sarah struggled to believe that Jones had once been a policeman, albeit the renegade kind with finely tuned powers of observation. Patrick pushed through the group of them, so excited he was scarcely in control of his voice. It descended to a whisper and ascended to a shriek in the course of a sentence and phrases spilled out everywhere stumbling over themselves.

'I've got it,' he yelled. 'I gottit. What this exhibition gonna be about – I gottit! S'all about murder and guilt, innit? That'll get them in.'

He hugged Di and took up a seat at the table. He was still young enough to hug without self-consciousness; still small enough to sit close and long may that last.

'All about what?' Sarah said.

'Stories,' he said, growling, hamming it up. 'All about stories. Murder and guilt is it. Yuk. That's what we like in films.'

'Be specific,' Sarah said, crisply. Her approach to children was to speak to them as adults, not ignoring their ideas but pinning them down. Patrick looked at her and calmed a little. He liked her enough, and regarded her with greater veneration since he had seen her without clothes, although he always loved her clothes. Sarah was colour. She was OK. He counted his fingers.

'Right. What I mean is, like what Di told me, think about it. Going to exhibit these paintings and they're all good paintings, I reckon. If you do it, and you want to get in kids like me, there's gotta be a link, a theme, a whatdo-youcallit. A story. Like something you've seen on the telly. You got to get them guessing. So, you make a story and you choose the paintings that go with that story. Faces, portraits. Faces telling their own story. Get it?'

'No,' Sarah said, carefully. 'I haven't got it. Convince me.'

Di was intensely interested and kept silent. Peg hovered. Jones went out the back and started supper.

'Secrets,' Patrick whispered, stabbing the table. 'Concentrate on those faces that have secrets and you know what? They all do, or I think so. So, thirty faces is the first exhibition. It's going to be called A Question of Guilt. Which of these faces is guilty and what are they guilty of? Which one could do a murder? Kids will love it.'

They were silent round the table and he was undeterred, impatient with their incomprehension and Di's suddenly pale face.

'Doesn't have to be murder. Look,' he said, patiently, his voice now at normal tone since they were so dim and failing to get the concept. 'You make the exhibition into a maybe detective story. You have all these faces, like, most of them worried-looking, cos nobody smiles for a portrait, and you got lots of non-smiling people and you say, is this one a murderer? Is this one a witness? Is this one hiding? Is this one in another room, hearing what's going on? Is this one looking sideways, cos he'd rather not see? Or is this one nodding to a friend and is this one just looking around to see who else is there? I mean, they'll all be at the same party in the same house, doing different stuff, and when you come through the door, you have to guess what they're all thinking. From the faces. And you have labels on the paintings, saying what you think they're like, what part they have in the story ... like whether they're nice or nasty ... are they a thief, could they be a detective, have they got a guilty conscience about something, even something small, and ... and the people who come in can say, no I don't agree. I don't agree with that. It would make them look closely, give them something to find in the pictures. Something to disagree with. Something to make them think about the painting and see them differently.'

His voice had risen an octave, descended back. The way it did when he was the centre of attention, which he surely was and not explaining his idea as well as he wanted.

'I think I'm beginning to get it,' Sarah said, glancing sideways at Di. 'Way to go. All the portraits are going to be possible characters in a crime drama or book, right? Give us an example of what you mean. Choose one picture.'

He clicked his fingers. 'Follow me.'

Meekly, they all followed him upstairs to the big room as if he was a tour guide.

'There,' Patrick said. One of my faves. Madame de Belleroche. She looks wicked, doesn't she? Like she could give you a look that would make you drop dead. But you know what? She's really, really nice. She talks to me.'

'"Swagger portrait of stylish, insouciant Edwardian woman with indistinct features, lounging in an elegant chair in a corseted dress, wearing a dressy hat. Imperiously beckoning to an audience. English Impressionist."' Di said, quoting from her own notes.

The figure leaned back, languid, with a tiny waist and a steely spine. At the same time, it always seemed that she beckoned forward, saying, come to me. Madame de B always had pride of place, always managed to have the spotlight, however things were arranged. She was the first painting Di had seen in this house, first when she came in with her mother, as a child, and then later, when she came to steal. The only painting ever to have been stolen. Madame de Belleroche always made her want to curtsy.

'Nice? She doesn't speak to me,' Sarah said. 'I find her a bit haughty. Stuck up. Got no time for anyone.'

'Wrong!' Patrick said, shaking his head. 'She's a lovely, lovely granny. Good with children. Watches over everyone. Listens to children, lets them hide around her. Under her skirts if they need. Wouldn't tick you off if she saw you smoking.'

'You know what?' Peg said, joining in, 'I see a nasty old bitch trying to control. She's on the edge of the party, right? No one's paying attention and she's sulking. Food's not been right and she's looking for someone to take her home.'

'Who says she's old?' Sarah said. 'You can't tell from her face and she's got a great figure. The pose is provocative. I don't think she's at a party, I think she's in a studio and she's just put her clothes back on after posing in the nude. There's another picture behind that. She's got plenty to be guilty about, though. Could be a duchess or a high class hooker.'

She looks a little like you, Di thought fondly. It was turning into an argument about which painting was nice, nasty, old, young or guilty.

'You see what I mean?' Patrick appealed to Di. 'You put up an exhibition of paintings, mainly faces, and write captions, saying what YOU think this person is like, what they're guilty about. You make them into a cast of characters. I reckon people always read the captions first. Then they look at the painting. And they bring what they know, and what they want the person to be like. Oh I don't know. Makes them realise there's dozens of ways of looking.'

'And I suppose,' Sarah said, warming to the theme, 'for this exhibition we need range. Bit players as well as stars. Some villains, some observers, thieves and sinners, detectives, a bit of high life and an example of low cunning. Accomplices, possibly a psychopath.'

'What I thought,' Patrick said,

'Need a policeman too,' Jones said, coming in from behind. 'And a Judge. Maybe a priest. Supper's ready.'

Di looked around this large and beautiful room, heard the buzz of voices talking across one another, and felt a moment of fairly pure happiness. Thomas would have loved this. Thomas Porteous loved parties and the idea of his beloved portraits being turned into an exhibition of various characters in a drama would have been the sort of thing he'd have come up with.

'We'll go back to it after supper,' Patrick said.

They left the quiet elegance of the grand room just as the light was fading and the lights from boats in the Channel began winking in the distance. No one had missed Saul.

'Do you know where old Toby lived?' Sarah asked Jones on the way downstairs. He looked at her curiously.

'Back of town. Think it's Dixon Avenue. Otherwise known as Arson alley. A million miles from here, love. At least a million miles.'

CHAPTER THREE

There was nothing elegant or spacious about the pebble-dashed, semi-detached house occupied by old Toby, the painter. It belonged in a street at the back of town as far away from the sea as it could get, and the whole road in which it lived looked as if it had turned its back on the world. They were cheap-build houses from the fifties, showing signs of wear and tear, apart from the tiny minority at one end gallantly maintained with double glazing and painting. It made for a varied street, Saul said to himself, surprised by the variety in this unfamiliar territory. Not a place to find a person of taste; the sort of street where you might find garden gnomes and water features at the front of the first house on the corner, and then, ten doors down-hill, an abandoned fridge, several dead bicycles, and a burned-out car. A place with empty houses, where few houses aspired and others had lost the will to live.

Old Toby's front yard, big enough for car or pond, was concrete with weeds round the edges, and his front door was hidden from the main road by a high privet hedge in a T shape, completely screening his entrance. An alley led to the back. Saul was happy about the high hedge, because while he had no scruples about what he was doing, it was nevertheless better to be unobserved.

What *was* he doing? Saul was unsure of anything other than his hunting instinct that told him Toby could paint and draw and it followed that his mean little house might hold good paintings, simple as that. It might contain things of which collectors dreamed. The work of an artist died with him as often as not, unless there was someone to carry the flame, and that would certainly be true of Toby Hanks, who had long since forgotten that he might once have owned a dog or a relative; illness did that. Toby might have forgotten most things except the use of his trembling hands. He might have been a collector himself. Artists often were. He himself might be worth collecting, judging by what Saul had seen. Nothing else mattered.

The house, entered from the front, was on the right side of hygiene, but only just, passing filth by a whisper. It smelled of old man and dog, with an occupant still making an effort. No piles of dirty dishes; pots and pans not quite washed, swiped with a dirty cloth and put away, the whole kitchen area longing for a brutal dose of bleach. Not quite yet the place for putting on a face mask, although certainly a case for gloves, and Saul, who was as fastidious as he was observant, trod cautiously. Tobacco, soap, semi-washed clothes were prevailing smells. Toby went out to smoke in the Life class and for sure he lived alone; no woman or man shared this place.

Bathroom little-used and rudimentary. Saul bypassed that and began at the top. He loved hidden places, particularly those between the ceilings and the roof; addicted to the very idea of an attic hiding place which fired his imagination. For a cause like this, he was willing to get dirty. At the top of this house, he put his head through a tiny trap door to find a dusty, empty space. So, he had begun at the top and worked down when really he should have gone the other way. Silly; Toby, with his dicky heart, would never have lugged stuff up here. Saul worked his way down, through strangely uncluttered rooms, and in the downstairs room, at the back, struck silver, if not gold.

This room would have been the scullery of the house, next to the back kitchen. Not a good room to use as a studio since the window was small and the light poor, but that was what it once was. A long time since anyone worked here: it seemed that Toby painted elsewhere and brought the work back, stored it in here, with some kind of order. This little room at the back of the house was invisible from the street in front and from the yard behind, with the window obscured by ivy. Saul fumbled for the light switch inside the door, found himself blinded by a daylight bulb, which bathed the place in blue. Yes, a studio once, with the kind of lighting that mimicked a midday sunlight and was beloved of artists who painted after dark to complete work done by day.

He heard a car pull up in the street outside, brakes squealing, doors slamming. There was the sound of a screaming argument between a woman and a man. Saul turned out the light, a reflex action. The argument outside escalated and then descended to shouting without blows struck, a front door crashed and the semi-silence resumed. Saul turned on the light again and began to look properly. How foolish to be perturbed in this invisible room, but the row reminded him of the nature of Toby's neighbours. Philistines, for sure. If there was anything to take, he should take it and take it now.

Toby had marshalled his works on paper on a large, home-made wooden structure, keeping them off the damp floor at least. Saul was grateful for small mercies. He began to sort through the stack of stiff paper, quickly found sketches, watercolour and pen, unfinished, possibly by more than one hand, could feel the ebbing of the adrenalin that had got him this far. He paused to mop his brow and look around and it was then his eyes lit on the twelve small paintings in frames ranged around the wall, standing on newspaper. They had their faces to the wall, so that he had not noticed them at first. All he could see was plain, brown-backed framed things with prominent labels, looking as if they might have been returned from somewhere else.

Saul turned round the nearest, then the next and the next, and sank to his knees, the better to look. Fine quality of paint, old and wonderful. Not clean, which was good, unseen for years, possibly older than old Toby himself. The paintings of his extreme youth or, more likely, not by him at all. Quality frames, indicating that someone had considered them valuable, labels on the reverse which he did not pause to inspect. Even in this remorseless, artificial daylight, reflecting immaculately unrestored, dirty surfaces, the quality made him whistle. Twelve small paintings, in perfect scale, making him long for more.

He could not leave them here; it was out of the question, a no-brainer. They needed rescue, *now*, there was no other choice. Look at the condition in which these were kept, look at it! He began to remove each of the framed paintings, two at a time, until he had stacked them all by the front door. A dozen. Then he opened the door and removed them to rest against the privet hedge by the gate. Still a dozen. Closed the door again and phoned for his special minicab. While he waited, he watched the paintings through the dirty glass of the half-glazed door, never taking his eyes off them. Fifteen minutes, the man said. Saul went back to the front room where Toby had a table full of paperwork. No computer, a heavyweight phone. Saul went to look at the sketches in the far room, but could not linger a moment longer, desperate to be gone. He waited outside, listening to the sounds of the street. Darkness was falling. None of the neighbours would know that Toby was dead, yet. Only when they did, would they think to descend.

The driver arrived in his clapped-out car, audible from half a mile away. He was a man of few words, Saul's favourite kind since he did not want to be known and did not care who knew him. This man never asked questions or queried who or what he carried and always had a cap down over his eyes, the better to see no evil or hear it either.

Saul removed the pictures from behind the privet hedge and put half into the boot of the taxi, with the rest going into the back seat. They sailed away without obser-vation.

'Good evening,' Saul said.

'Good?' the man said. 'What's so good about it? Didn't think I'd ever see you down this end, someone like you; this end's where they burn cars and houses.'

'Really,' Saul murmured. 'Oh dear.'

When they got back to the old schoolhouse, where the man had delivered Saul many a time before, he helped unload. The pictures were not heavy. It took a few minutes for Saul to get them up to the front door of Di's house and sneak them inside. Saul was small, with remarkable dexterity when it came to handling paintings. He paid the generous tip for silence and assistance and considered the next problem. He still did not want to be observed.

The new front door closed sweetly behind him. On his way through, Saul could tell there was some kind of party going on in the big room upstairs. Echoes of laughter. Oh God, the exhibition conference – but good: time to spare. A matter of five more minutes to take all the paintings through the kitchen and down into the glorious cellar. Di wouldn't be going there any time soon. He was sweating and exhausted and wired. Then he went upstairs, dusting himself down, to greet the frivolous multitudes.

'None of these people are smiling,' Peg was saying. 'Does that mean the model's feeling guilty? You got so many non-smiling people on these walls. A load of miseries.'

'Wash your mouth out, you.' This was Patrick's shrill, breaking voice. 'They aren't miserable, they're thinking. *You* don't smile when you model.'

'No, it doesn't mean *misery*.' Saul heard the patient, amused tones of his sister, Sarah. 'It means that smiles are difficult to sustain. I mean, who can keep smiling long enough for someone to paint the smile? You'd go into spasm. Your face muscles can't do it. You can't sit smiling for hours. Try it.'

Silence followed, punctuated by giggles. When Saul

came in, they were all wearing fixed grins, perma-smiles, the sort he wore when going round a craft fair or an opening night when he thought the paintings were shit. All of them experimenting with keeping a smile on a face like a series of salesmen. They looked ridiculous until they collapsed.

'Time it,' Sarah was saying. 'It's about a minute, max. After that, you have to let it go.'

Patrick, whose face had been contorted into an unconvincing grimace that made him look like a monkey holding its breath and baring teeth, relaxed with a whoomph, and fell down. They were all overexcited, Saul thought; not drunk, merely exhilarated. Even Peg, with whom Saul had an uneasy relationship because as far as he could see she only liked oil paintings because they were easy to dust and difficult to damage. Peg, in the meantime, had forgotten how much she reacted to the paintings on the walls, how it was, having landed in this strange house, they were a part of it. How much she was allowed to speak her mind, now she was a model with all the authority that came from that. A beautiful model.

'I get it,' she was saying. 'You can't keep up a smile. So every bugger looks either serious or shifty. Like the way you do when you put on your make-up in the morning. Or shave, or summat. Don't smile into mirrors, do we? And nobody asks us models to smile, 'cause they know. And anyway, it would really put them off. Models are supposed to look mournful or recently fucked, sorry, Patrick.'

It went on, the impossibility of smiling. People pulling faces. Trying out expressions, mournful, hilarious, and grave. Peg could wiggle her eyebrows. Saul stayed in the background, thinking to himself, *Those paintings I've put in the basement can't possibly be recent ones by Toby Hanks, the frames are wrong. I wish I'd taken some of the sketches; I'm going to need them. Why do I think the paintings have been taken down from an exhibition, or a gallery? Because of the labels on the back that I haven't looked at yet. Can't do it now, when will I get the chance? When Di goes to London. I want to see them properly before I tell her. Then she'll understand. Need the sketches. What are they talking about?* Saul shook himself awake, aware that he was mercifully ignored, and that much had been achieved in his absence.

'Next,' Sarah said. 'Captions, please.'

They moved on to a tiny picture by Gwen John, which was always kept in a shady corner out of the light, because the pigment was fragile. A woman in profile, with a hat and fur scarf, sitting in a French church, huddling for warmth. An intimate sketch, a little self-portrait of a woman, sitting.

'Weird,' Peg said. 'What's she doing?'

'Queuing to go to confession,' Sarah said. 'That's in the title. She wants to confess. She had an obsession with a sculptor, Rodin, didn't she?'

'But it isn't a painting *of* her, it's a painting *by* her,' Di said. 'Don't get confused. What do you think *she's* like?

The person in the painting, not the artist. What do you think? Look at her and say what you think of *her*.'

Jones squinted at it, put on his spectacles, moved closer.

'Sweet little old lady?' he said. 'I don't think so. All huddled up and no central heating but she isn't even old. She's just come in for a warm-up. She'd rob you blind, that one, and you wouldn't even notice. Drug smuggler, that's her. You wouldn't notice her coming through Customs with a kilo of heroin under that hat.'

'She's an observer,' Saul said. 'An observer of people.'

'Ah, there you are,' said Jones. 'Where've you been?'

'Nowhere,' Saul said.

'You been trespassing again?' Peg said. Joking, seeing dust on his clothes.

'Of course not.'

'Next,' Di said.

'Now here's one,' said Peg. '"Woman in roll neck jumper, smoking. Circa 1960s." Adrian Ryan.'

'Got a caption for her,' Sarah said. 'She's an adulteress, doesn't know whether to murder her husband or her lover, neither of whom love her.'

'Nah,' Jones said. 'She's a bored person in a pub waiting for the next round of drinks. Son's just been arrested.'

Next: Society portrait of Juliet Strachey, niece of a famous uncle, painted by a noted artist of the time, Anthony Devas. Hair done to a turn, wearing black gloves and lace, cupid bow mouth, bosom decorated with a gardenia.

'She was the business,' Jones said. 'Looks calculating, stares you straight in the eye. Die, she says, die now. Save time.'

'I don't see it,' Sarah said. 'I think she's lonely, dressing up to hide. Or she may be a jewel thief, after someone else's diamonds.'

'You gottit, you gottit, you gottit!' Patrick burst out. 'You got the idea!'

'Say it again, honey,' Peg said. 'What idea was that?'

'This is what we do to make this exhibition work,' Patrick said. 'Get people to look. We put up the paintings and next to them put up a description of what kind of character they'd be if they were in a murder story. Give each one a role, a part, just like we've been doing. Say, this one's guilty, this one's innocent. Invite people to disagree, make up their own version. Makes them look for guilt and secrets and people they know. So,' he said, turning to Di with his big hands on his skinny hips. 'Which ones do we choose?'

'We choose the ones that go with the theme,' Di said. 'We choose faces and expressions and scenes that can be interpreted in all sorts of ways, depending where you're coming from.'

Saul watched what he would call a deeply unserious approach to art. He was seeing yet again what Thomas Porteous had seen in Diana Quigly, including her capacity for delight. Thomas would have approved thoroughly. And all the same, he felt for the key to Toby's house which remained in his pocket. The dog with the big head came and sniffed him and then laid itself across his feet, with the unerring instinct of an animal approaching a human who does not like it. It had worked with Peg and not yet with Saul, though this time he surprised himself by stroking her ears. How cool and silky they were, rather beautiful.

Patrick was thinking of going home to his mother tomorrow and what he had to do beforehand and went a bit quiet, but hey, all this was his idea and they loved it, and he was proud of himself, so he cheered up again. At least Di was coming with him. There would be that interlude on the train before he faced the cross-examination of his envious parents. In the morning, he would take photos of the basement as his father had asked. That way, they might not be as angry. It depressed him that they used him as a spy. He looked sideways at Di. She smiled at him.

Di remembered that she was going to London with Patrick, and she would see Steven. Wished he was here, listening in, and laughing.

Sarah caught her brother's eye, and he shook his head. She worried for them all.

She had the distinct impression that Di knew very well who had pushed her on the cliff.

In Dixon Avenue, a man who was tired from a long walk on the cliffs stood back from the window of his semi-detached house. There was no point standing there and waiting for anyone to come back next door. No one would come back tonight. Not Toby, or that bastard thief, but at least he knew where the thief had gone, so it could be worse.

He shed an awkward tear for Toby, although he was not a crying man.

Toby had made him look handsome.

Chapter Four

Picture. *Train coming into crowded station, with clock above.*

Di and Patrick were on the train before anyone else was functioning. Patrick had been up first, detouring to the basement with his phone to take photos, something he'd left to the last minute because he felt so obscurely guilty about it. *Tell me everything*, his mother Gayle would say, and one way and another, he would. He had been there for a whole fortnight and it was never quite enough. Di would go with him as far as the station in London.

Both of them loved the train; it was where they had some of the best conversations. An hour and a half of high-speed liberation, a place for confidential, random talking and quiet excitement in the journey. An example of how much better it could be to travel safely rather than arrive.

'I'd like to go in the driver's cab,' Patrick said, with his nose pressed to the window. 'See everything from the front. I want to see the tunnels opening up in front of me, feel like a rocket, going to crash, *whiz*.'

Di wanted to make it happen; she would make it happen. She wanted the world for Patrick and she hated his ambivalence about going home. Patrick loved the parents who neglected him and he liked the London in which he lived, but he never felt as safe there as he did in his grandfather's house by the sea, or even as safe as he felt on this train. Patrick's mother Gayle, the daughter of Thomas, was a bitter and unpredictable woman with a greedy failure of a husband. Both of them had assumed that when Thomas Porteous died, he would leave his fortune and his collection to his two daughters, Gayle and Beatrice. They had assumed it although they had despised him and when everything was left to Di, the violence of their reaction had been extreme. They had been persuaded by Saul to collect paintings from the basement and instead, vandalised the house in a frenzy of greed. That ignominious episode and Gayle's attack on Di was supposedly captured on CCTV cameras, making them blackmailable. Di was not proud of this insurance policy. The paintings they had been encouraged to take had realised them a quarter of a million pounds, but that would never be sufficient. They could not contest the Porteous will as long as they thought there was evidence of that night. Nor could they prevent Patrick from his holiday visitations.

Two years on, the hatred still bubbled with Gayle and Edward, but Patrick had always loved his grandfather and latterly, Di, and it came to suit his parents to farm him off to the seaside as often as he wished. Otherwise, he would have run there. Let him get what he could out of the mess: let Di buy his clothes and feed him. Di Porteous had a strange non-relationship with Patrick's parents. They hated her, blamed her, reviled her and envied her, yet, when it came to the care of their son, trusted her absolutely. Di sent Patrick back with small gifts for his mother: flowers, soap, things like that, to reinforce in his eyes the legend of their mutual forgiveness and respect, but nothing was forgiven or forgotten, nothing at all.

And Edward had pushed her.

When Patrick went home, he would be cross-examined about everything that happened in his grandfather's house and he would reply with plentiful omissions. He might tell them the house was falling down and show them a sketch of Di looking ugly. Gayle liked that. Patrick was used to keeping secrets, but Di knew he could not keep them all, nor should he. Except on the train. Talking on the train was like people talking on the doorstep at the end of the party, saying things they had meant to say earlier and forgotten. Or like talking when looking at paintings or the sea. *Oh, I meant to tell you;* sometimes a sudden rush of information.

'Why did Mum hate Grandpa?' Patrick asked. 'How could anyone hate Grandpa?'

'Your mother was told lies about him for a very long time,' Di said carefully. 'Don't think she hates him now.'

She hates me, though.

Patrick was sketching in his notebook, one hand scribbling while he stared through the window. He was nervous and optimistic at the same time.

'She's not so bad, my mum,' he said.

'Of course she's not. Oh look, here's the big long tunnel, the last one. Did I tell you about the time when Grandpa and I came up to London in the driver's cab?'

'You never did!'

'Yes, we did. Thomas knew a train driver who'd been a boy he taught in school, and, there we were, all the way, in the cab.'

And then they were crowding out of the train, running to the barrier, putting in tickets the wrong way round and getting stuck, getting through to the other side for the last of the very big hugs that Di relished, while thinking about what really went on in his London flat and knowing that she could not ask. At least there had been no bruises when he arrived this last time and at least she had other limited sources of information from Steven.

'By the way,' Patrick said in a throwaway line, 'look out for what Saul put in the basement last night. He was down there, last thing. He's up to something.'

'And you were down there, first thing. What are you?' she said, laughing. 'My spy?'

'I'm your best mate. And another thing I forgot to tell you. You know Dad's friend, Steven, who's your friend, too, but Dad doesn't know that, well, he comes round, sometimes. The man who was on the boat when we went to the Goodwin Sands. He comes round for a drink, talks to me a lot and I quite like him, really. He likes to talk about drawings; he likes the ones I do, that Steven. Said he'd like to take me out, round galleries and stuff. Should I go?'

'Oh yes, see everything you can. Think about the exhibition, will you? And don't worry about the paintings Saul put in the basement. I know all about it.'

Not quite true. She knew where Saul had gone the evening before, after the death in the class, because Sarah had warned her. She had looked, briefly, long before dawn, seen the labels of things turned to the wall, and controlled her anger. She knew what the labels described, but there were priorities and coming to London with Patrick came first.

'That's alright then. Good,' Patrick said.

'Phone me?'

'You bet.'

The rush of information was over and he wanted to be off. She watched him scamper down the escalator, relieved how he did not pause to wave back, already on to the next thing. A boy who protected his mother, whom he did not resemble at all. His grandfather's child, with the same tastes and instincts, an artist in the making, perhaps. A pawn in a game that might be escalating. Dear God, if she was in a position to blackmail them, they were also in a position to blackmail her with this still child she loved so much.

In the twenty minutes it took to walk to her next destination, Di was thinking of Patrick being an artist and hoped not. The life of the dedicated artist, according to history, anecdote and jokes, was not tranquil. Obsessive-compulsive perfectionists, with lousy relationships, so rumour had it; possibly never resigned to anything, doomed to disappointment and frustration, pursuing a vision forever out of reach with only occasional triumphs. Suitable profession for a manic depressive or a plain depressive, since added creativity always seemed to go with someone on the way up or the way down. *I'd rather be collector than creator*, Thomas had said; *I prefer my own delusions. Let Patrick draw for pleasure and become a train driver.* Di laughed at herself for succumbing to clichés and went to meet the man who thought he was her brother. Patrick's dad's friend Steven. Who, among other things, looked out for Patrick. How complicated it all was.

*

Steven Cockerel loved heights. He was a city man, a well-educated chancer made good, prematurely rich for his relatively young age. A man who could segue from ruthlessness to kindness and often got the two confused. Emotionally retarded, some would say: too much money too soon and easily bored, before he began collecting art. Definitely a closet thief, reformed. Collecting was a curse and a joy. By the time he had discovered that art was a lousily uncertain investment, he was addicted, and it infuriated him. As soon as his unreliable emotions were engaged with a painting, he lost the cutting edge of his bargaining power and fell into lust. He was like a star-struck lover, buying jewels for an unsuitable woman. Lust turned to love and recklessness, and then he met Diana Porteous, who turned him into a true collector, led by his heart and his eyes. These days, he only wanted what made his heart sing; bugger the value. *I am not a nice man*, he often told himself. *It is Diana and her paintings that have redeemed me and I shall never steal again.* But even so, there has to be method in madness.

His heart sang now. They met on Blackfriars Bridge: they always met on bridges; they were impelled to meet by water and both of them were addicted to the sea. Like Thomas had been, like Patrick and Jones were, and Saul and Peg were not. They had more than that in common. Steven had grown up in the next village to that of Thomas Porteous's schoolhouse; it was in his blood; he had been there as a child and that was where he may have inhaled a latent love of paintings. He was a bastard child, begat by his father of a local girl and adopted by his father's wife as her own. He had grown up in the belief of belonging, while never belonging at all. Steven's moral compass, as well as his ability to relate to fellow humans, were, as he put it himself, skewed. Somewhere on the autistic scale, Saul had drawled; he's insanely acquisitive and profoundly untrustworthy. Di didn't think so. She alone could tease him about his obsessive characteristics since, after all, she shared some of them.

Steven wanted to believe that the local girl by whom he was begat was Di's mother, rather than the teenage cleaner in his father's country house. So they were possible half-siblings, with the same long-dead mama. The dates fitted; the belief suited him; he wanted it to be true. Di's mother's name was not on his birth certificate. Whatever the truth, Steven and Di had a remarkable affinity, uncanny things in common. She had recognised his dark side and brought it into the light. Their first meetings had been extraordinary and inauspicious, pushing them to fight tooth and nail, and the result was a peculiar mutual understanding that was maybe a result of blood being thicker than water, maybe not. His face lit up when he saw her; the sight of her made him shine.

'Hello, sister,' he said. 'Do we have to meet like this?'

'Your call,' she said, so patently pleased to see him it

made him want to shout. Her capacity for forgiveness was better than his. He had stolen from her, thrown darts at her and all she could say was that was just what might have happened if they had been brother and sister growing up together.

They might have bitten and snarled and eaten each other's toys, while as it was when they met, they talked endlessly, sensitive to each other, and in the absence of meeting, emailed. Protective of one another. They were both collectors, surely the biggest bond of all, thicker than blood.

'Why do we meet like this?' he said. 'Is it because your ersatz family don't approve of me? Dear Saul, the redoubtable Sarah? To say nothing of Jones, who would like to throw me off the pier.'

'You exaggerate,' Di said, 'but then you always do. One of many things I like about you. We meet here because it suits us and you live here.'

'I'm mightily relieved you like anything about me,' he said, taking her arm and walking her back across the bridge, with Westminster in the distance. 'And I quite understand why the rest of your clan find me so suspicious.'

'They don't trust you, is all. Come to think of it, neither do I.'

But I know you. And I trust you, thought Steven.

'How healthy,' he said. 'I don't trust anyone either.' *Except you.*

They walked on, comfortably arm in arm, both the same height, well weighted to each, both small persons.

'Thank you,' she said, 'for looking out for Patrick.'

'Not difficult,' Steven said. 'You know I was at school with his father, you know all the rest. They think I'm a friend and they love to hang around anyone rich. They tell me things; I drink with them, I go round their house. And you asked me to look out for him, and so I do. You know, don't you, that I would do anything for you? Sister?'

She stopped. They were on the wrong side of the bridge for the grander view.

He paused to look at the water, looking away from her although he wanted to look at her all the time.

'Why's that, Steven? Why do you do it? What's in it for you? Is it because we might have the same DNA? Or do you think young Patrick might be a good investment?'

'Oh yes, I'm always after a good investment. No, it's because it's in the stars,' he said. 'It's because I like you better than anyone I've ever met. You've changed me. OK, I'm not comfortable, I'm out of my zone, I don't know what's happened to me, but there we go. I'd do anything for you. And I really like that boy. I'd like to take him out to see paintings.'

'I once read that if two people meet over a painting, it has to be a romance,' Di said.

'Romance? What's that? The love of art, of course, is what brought us together, sister mine,' he said, with artificial gravity. 'Only the higher planes of art appreciation, of course. And the fact that we may both have learned the hard way that it is basically wrong to steal. On that note, I want to talk about Winifred Doris and her emails, and her missing pictures. Thought of little else ever since I looked up the Kemsdown collection in the Mellon Library. It was once a fine collection.'

'So you know what *should* be in Winifred's museum?'

'Yes, I know what should be there, but not what isn't. It's thrown up a whole lot of ideas. I don't mean "thrown up". Perhaps I mean "refreshed".'

They walked on, her arm warm against his.

Love of a kind. Intense liking, at least. Later, when they were sitting down, they were talking even faster.

'OK, let me tell you what I'm doing,' Steven said. 'I'm not quite the leopard who has changed spots for moral stripes. I want terrific, forgotten paintings, but I want them at the best price. So, inspired by Winifred Doris, I'm investigating galleries with fantastic holdings of paintings that lie mouldering in the dark, doing nothing. You know that, it was you who suggested it.'

He leaned towards her, touching her hand over the table. His blue eyes were pale in the sunlight and he looked earnestly fanatical until he grinned.

'Someone invites you to steal,' he said, slowly. 'And by dint of that, opens up another route.' He tapped the printed email. 'Seems to me, reading between the lines of this, the current Director of Winifred Doris's museum would love to get rid of the old dross in the store, especially if it meant money being freed up for innovation. So, I wrote to the Director that Dorothy so despises, requesting to look at the paintings of a particular artist they don't have on show. A down-in-the-stores artist. I shall pursue him, as one ambitious man to another, if you see what I mean. Maybe he might be amenable to getting rid of old paintings that are a burden to his ambitions, just like he'd like to get rid of Winifred, don't you think? He might find himself in a position to liberate them for a price. Fix it. That's my approach.'

'I see. Semi-theft. They don't belong to the Director. They belong to the public.'

'Who, as things stand, may never see them again?'

Their eyes met.

'I'm more worried by someone being bullied. Winifred Doris.'

'Shall I continue?' he asked. 'See what I can do? I need your approval.' She leaned forward, not granting it, not yet by any means, but intrigued by this version of him.

'I thought this might be an approach that could be rolled out,' Steven said, 'to archives, museums. Legal acquisitions of anything visual surplus to requirement. Stuff they don't want.'

'Ambitious,' Di said. 'Tell me, when you first wrote to this Director, which artist was it you were asking to see?

Was there just the one? I was asking about Disher and got back that letter from Winifred. Who were you asking about?'

'I was asking about someone called Toby, possibly Tobias Hanks, signs as TH. Not a name to conjure with. Born 1930. I'd think an anglicised name, rather than a real one. They look more European than English somehow. Very little information on him. Exhibited rarely, scarcely known. Listed as acquired by the Kemsdown in 1960. TH painted people from behind, looking over the shoulder, empty rooms, like Edward Hopper, Vilhelm Hammershøi. Brilliant, not famous. Can't see this Director having much time for them. I emailed the Director, called Mr Cloake, by the way, who has three times failed to reply.'

'TH,' Di said. 'Toby Hanks.'

'Could be known as,' Steven agreed. 'Always signs TH.'

She began to laugh, softly, almost whistling.

'Toby Hanks,' she repeated. 'Toby Hanks. TH.'

'I want these paintings,' Steven said. 'I desperately want to see them and bring them into the light. What do you think?'

'Yes,' she said, computing the whole history. *Toby Hanks, not local man, aged approximately eighty-four.*

'So let me tell you a story,' Di said. 'A man called Toby, lived at the other end of the town, in the bad bit where I was born. I never knew him, or knew he was a painter. He died, yesterday, during a painting class. Chronic heart condition, old. Saul spotted his work in the class, said it was outstanding.'

She stopped there, because she didn't know enough to continue with the next episode. Didn't know the detail of what Saul had placed in the basement and she had merely glimpsed in a bleary, preoccupied dawn. He sensed her hesitation.

'Coincidence,' he said, folding his white hand over her brown one. 'Please don't tell me. Not my business. Where do we go from here ?'

'We promise to speak or write every day,' Di said, staring at his fingers, as if examining his nails. 'That's what we do. We share information, is what. We behave honourably, we pursue, we collaborate.'

'Ah, yes,' he said. 'That's what we do.'

She would be lonely when she left him, he to go to his eyrie and she to the high-speed train. *Toby Hanks, TH, aged eighty-four. Maybe resident in the cellar.* Also thinking that as long as Steven believed he was her brother, she had his attention; she had some control, though there was nothing of her mother in him, nothing about the eyes, the nose, and the mouth. There was the devil in him, though, and the devil was rising in her.

'Shall I persist?' he had said. 'Shall I pursue this?'

'Yes, yes. And I shall see if it could be the same artist. And I shall write to Winifred Doris.'

They parted, waving. He strode away, with his

purposeful walk, could not resist turning back, just as she did, both catching each other turning to look, reluctant to lose sight, waving again.

Steven walked fast, sidestepping crowds, longing to get on that train and go to the sea with her. He had never submitted those samples of her blood and his for the sort of test which might prove a sibling relationship. He said he would, but hadn't, for fear of a definitive answer he did not want. There was no proof that he and Di shared the same DNA. As long as she believed she was his half-sister, she would surely continue to want to know him. If they were not remotely related, he could not imagine why on earth she would, or at least not until he had earned her respect. Steven Cockerel had no faith in his ability to keep a friend and did not consider himself a likeable man. Nor did it occur to him that he might be loved simply for what he was without his money. Love must be earned. Maybe she would love him for what he did, like him when he proved himself and earned his spurs. She would love him if he befriended Patrick; if they joined forces and brought things into the light, forged their collections honourably and helped each other.

He consulted the screen that was his window on the world to find an email from the Director of Kemsdown.

Paintings by TH under restoration. Try next year.

Brusque, evasive, brief, dismissive. Which was quite unlike the email that arrived for Di Porteous.

CHAPTER FIVE

Dear Mrs Porteous,

Thank you for your kind response. I hope you don't mind my writing like this. It was good of you to enquire about me.

Winifred Doris Smith is my name. Otherwise known as Winnie or Dot, while Mr Cloake calls me Whiny or Dotty. I had an official title, which is Head of Collections, Kemsdown Museum. I am not an artist myself, but hold the true ones in the greatest respect. My brother is one; so was my mother.

There's no doubt at all about me being Dotty, answered to that name since I was seven. I go with the description on the tin. Mad as a snake, a box full of frogs, all that. 'Poor Dotty,' he addresses me, with his hand on my shoulder when the Trustees come round. 'Poor Dotty,' he says, 'she has so much responsibility. What would we do without her?' All that, while his hand leaves bruises on my bones. Sometimes he flicks his finger against the back of my head.

'Poor Dotty,' he says. 'She's been here a long time.'

So long, he means, that she's forgotten what's in the store, or so he hopes. The Director's mission statement is 'Cutting-edge art for the town', by which he means a cutting-edge reputation for himself that will get him further up the ladder. What he doesn't seem to realise is that he was probably hired to run the place down. There are virtually no staff left.

There's a rumbling upstairs. We are strangely arranged in this place. There are rather grand municipal offices downstairs, since we're housed in the Town Hall, where we have the top two floors, and they have the ground, where the Council Chamber is. I go right back to the dark ages when we had paintings on the walls.

As I said, we have the top two floors, and then we have the middle floor, about which no one knows much. Half a floor beneath. You reach it either by a tiny lift, or via the iron stairs. One section of this limited space is for stacked objects, i.e. things in transit, going on loan or coming back, then there's the main part which consisted of the perfectly designed hanging rails that you could pull in and out, allowing you to see everything in there. It was our policy that if a painting we owned was not on display, you could always go to the middle floor, pull it out and see it. A great way to store a lot of paintings and make them easy to view. All that. Mr Cloake removed the hanging rails to make space for his junk. Paintings are all over the place, coming out of the corners with no room to sort through them. He would prefer that this whole floor did not exist. It is our personal war zone.

I don't know if he's negotiating to sell the things or if he might be mixing things up to hide what's missing. He fends off the very few people who ask to view by saying the painting in question is out on loan, or being restored, try again next year. Or the stockroom is being refurbished. Researchers will settle for an image they can get elsewhere. No one is ever allowed to see.

Thinking of the store, I should tell you about the contents.

OK, we have too many of cows and horses. We have too many pictures donated by the burghers of the town, i.e., portraits of themselves, and we also have some superb twentieth-century paintings by artists who were never famous. We have marvellous things and indifferent things, but without putting them out on display, how do you know the difference? You put them out and let your public decide.

I know what the public like. They respond to quality of all kinds: they like things that draw them into another world; they make up their own minds. They don't like shit and they don't like being patronised. Our latest display, currently under deconstruction, is of a series of headless paper chickens, accompanied by a mission statement. The next exhibition is going to be an installation of lights. The place is dying and the paintings are in prison. Only the metal models, the dog and the waitress, have a semblance of life. Paintings need the minimum of words.

I am guarding the middle floor with my life, but if I stay down here any length of time, the Director sends for me. I can't disappear for hours, which is what I need to do in order to search through. Someone is coming downstairs. The stairs are made of iron and the footsteps are heavy. They go clank, clank, clank.

I am not a well woman, because I have a chronic disease of the heart, but I'm fit enough. Sorry to go

on for so long, but I shall be out of contact for a
week or two. I hope you will come soon after that,
now you know the geography. Remember the fire
door at the back that the smokers leave open.

I haven't described Mr Cloake; see picture on
website. Think of a vain man, so computer illiterate
he can't change his own password, with a penchant
for redheads.

That was the long email that greeted Di in the morning. Time of sending, two a.m. Dotty was a night bird.
The email address was not the museum. Di's acknowledging email came straight back.

The letter was shocking. Di forwarded it to Sarah and
Steven. Names haunted her: Toby Hanks, Kemsdown,
Winifred Doris, running together as if they rhymed. She
had glanced at the paintings in the basement, stacked
against the wall, only to see the old labels on the back.
Property of Kemsdown Museum. Now Saul was going to
unveil them.

They were standing in the cellar, Saul as always enjoying
its theatrical potential. He was not in any way repentant.
Looking at the cellar objectively, she could see how beautiful it was, how elegant the proportions and what a fine
space it provided now the vaulted roof rose above like a
blessing. She could see that Saul's restoration had been in

itself a work of art, yet she was ever uneasy down in these depths. The house was built on shingle: she had never seen the cellar in flood, but she knew that it had happened and it followed that it would happen again.

Where there was now a respectable entrance from the back, sloping down to the main space via elegant stairs, there had once been metal shutters which had been prised open to allow her small self to slip through in order to steal from the man of the house, the first time she ever came here. She could feel the sensation, now; fear, cold, an acute ability to notice the detail, and most of all, the ghastly exhilaration of the adolescent thief she had been. There were too many echoes. The acoustics were perfect. You could whisper in here and still be heard, while she wanted to yell, because to her, it was still a mausoleum. Saul, on the other hand, was indifferent to the nature of the sea and how ruthless it was; how swift and sometimes malicious. We had the best engineers, he said; it's been tanked out, rebuilt by specialists; it cost you a fortune, so it must be safe, OK?

They were having a face-off, with Sarah acting as referee.

'I didn't *steal* them,' Saul said. 'Not *as such*. I *liberated* them from a horrible little house in a back street of this benighted town. To save them from the neighbours who would have put them on a bonfire and been disappointed how slow they were to burn. How could I have left them there? In such surroundings? The man was dead already. They had to be rescued. I thought I did rather well.'

Collectors are close aligned to thieves, Sarah thought. Always that ambivalence. Di was both.

'This is my house,' Di said.

'And mine, in spirit,' Saul retorted. 'Or at least you always say so. But you don't mean it. You want my allegiance, my devotion to the collection, but you don't. Oh, I don't know. You don't want my *individuality*.'

'I admire you,' she said. 'But we don't always approve of what the other does. So, shall we look at what you liberated? And then discuss? Applying the moral and visual standards of Thomas Porteous, rather than our own?'

'Thomas was a rescuer of fine paintings, and he would have taken them,' Saul said, cunningly. 'I'm sure he would.'

'Not without establishing who owned them and not without paying, he wouldn't,' Di said. 'Shall we look?'

Saul had prepared the display. A dozen paintings face out, lined up against the wall. They looked as if they might have formed a sequence. All of them were interiors. First, the back view of a woman sweeping a wooden floor, her broom still, her hidden profile turned towards the open door of the room. The open door led on to another room, and another, where the light seemed littered with dust. The next, a woman sitting at a table, leaning back into the chair, restfully, possibly doing something with her invisible hands as she faced the wall and the light touched the upswept hair on the back of her neck.

Next, the back view of a man in an empty shop, seen as if the viewer was looking through the window as he examined what might have been a coin. People intent on activity, in places of subdued light. What could she call them? Everyday situations, everyone active and oblivious to scrutiny. People at work, no noise, no vibrant colour, no narrative. No full-on faces, but expressive backs, clothes you could stroke and warmth you could feel.

In the last two last of the twelve pictures as Saul had arranged them, the artist simply painted the rooms and left out the occupants. They made Di reach out and touch; they drew her in: they made retreat impossible. Here was sadness, mystery, contentment, quiet joys, hope and sorrows as if the onlooker was walking towards the light from the windows and finally, leaving. A sombre but intensely colourful palette, the finish sketchy and unpolished, as if there was more to do. Rooms within rooms.

'Sort of English Vermeer, eat your heart out,' Saul said. 'And absolutely unique. The paint and the provocation. Could paint like a dream, could even paint dreams. I can hear the creak of the floorboards, want to touch a shoulder. In one way, they're like a series of sleeping beauties.'

A woman, back to camera, reaching up to hang washing off a rail suspended from the ceiling in a kitchen, her face averted to the task and her stance alone suggesting she was singing. These were portraits of lives being lived, showing how much you could reveal without revealing the face and how much rooms revealed of their occupants. Figurative, yes, impressionistic, yes; totally absorbing and powerful, yes.

'And of course,' Saul was saying, busily, 'they are ever more extraordinary because of *when* they were painted. I'd have put these late nineteenth century, but they aren't. They're mid twentieth century, not the greatest heyday for stuff like this. But he isn't copying anyone, this man, whatever his influences. They're like Vermeer, but not Vermeer. More like Sickert, but not Sickert, though the same in the way of his small paintings, not epic, quite spectacular because they make you use your imagination.'

The paintings brought the space alive. Di yearned to see them in daylight.

'Nobody's posing,' Sarah said. 'They all seem to be unaware of being painted at all.'

Di was not listening. She was lost, smelling the canvas, asking questions, *how did he do this?* Did he put up an easel and paint on the spot, or did he make sketches and take them away to paint the painting? She did not realise she was muttering.

'I love them,' Saul said with unusual vehemence. 'I absolutely love them.'

Love was not a word Saul often employed. He recovered, quickly, moved into persuasive mode, although he could tell from Di's attitude that he was speaking to the converted.

'They would be a wonderful addition to this collection,' Saul said. 'We don't have enough from this generation of English artists. We've got hidden masterpieces, oh yes, but not this hidden master. They're also desperately unfashionable. And of course,' he added cunningly, 'they'd be perfect for the Question of Guilt exhibition.'

'I don't know why,' Sarah murmured, finding herself moved into an admiration zone she usually resisted, 'but I think of this artist as *she*, rather than *he*.'

'They don't belong to us,' Di said. 'They can't be part of the exhibition.'

'They didn't belong to Toby Hanks, either. Turn them round.'

Di moved down the row of paintings, turning them to face the wall, reluctantly. It seemed wrong to hide them again. It was dangerous for her to handle paintings she admired as much as these. The desire to own them, look after them, grew with the very act of looking. Saul watched her.

KEMSDOWN MUSEUM AND ART GALLERY.

'Bloody hell,' Sarah said.

'Now tell me that your husband would not have liberated these little masterpieces if given the chance,' he said.

'No, he wouldn't,' Di said. 'But I might have done.'

'Wait a minute,' Sarah. 'Are you sure we know who painted these things? Just because these paintings, signed TH, are found in our Toby's house, doesn't mean he painted them. They're nothing like what he painted in class.'

'True,' Saul said. 'They may not be by him at all. That's why we need the sketches.'

'What sketches?'

'The sketches still lingering in Toby's horrible house. A hundred or so. His own stuff. We need them for comparison. To establish if it's the same artist.'

Di thought of Steven. Wondered what Steven would have done. She was no longer angry with Saul, only in agreement. She looked again at the exhibition labels. *Kemsdown Museum and Art Gallery.*

'According to my researches,' Saul chanted, 'which have, by the way, occupied me vastly, a private donor gave all these paintings, by one TH and possibly at least twelve more, to this museum in 1960. TH had exhibited there once, in his lifetime. According to the flawed records of who owns what, the municipal museum still owns these paintings, plus more. But we can't know if *these* were painted by *our* Toby without researching the rest of *our* Toby's sketches and making comparisons. And they're still in his house.'

'We have to return these,' Di said. 'These have to go back to their rightful owners. We have to take them back to where they belong.'

'For sure,' Saul said, evenly. 'When we know who actually painted them and who actually owns them. So far we have a man who is dead and who might have painted them. Or stole them, or was given them? I need the sketches, and anyway, wouldn't it be nice to rescue the rest of *our* Toby's work before it goes up in smoke?'

He paused for effect.

'I thought that you and Sarah might go back to Toby's house. He's only been dead four days. The vandals might not have landed yet, although Jones tells me there was another fire further up the road, yesterday. I still have the key,' he murmured. 'I can't go back myself, but you two can. I gather Mr Hanks remains with the funeral directors, waiting for someone to claim him. Post inquest. He is, after all, dead, with no one to carry his flame.'

Sarah and Di looked at each other.

'I'm up for it,' Sarah said. 'Come on, Di. We'll do it like before. We'll make it official.'

So Di went back to being a thief.

By that early evening, nothing had changed in Dixon Avenue. Sarah Fortune's red hair was scratched back into a ponytail behind a cap with a peak. She and Di both wore yellow nylon jackets over black trousers, unflattering, but official. Sarah, who always drove as if in command of a tank, parked the white van in a road of several vehicles while talking loudly. She stood and smoked in the street, stubbed it out. *Smoking is bad for you.* 'Let's make it noisy,' she'd said. 'Let's not make it secretive and quiet, I hate all that. We've come to clean the man's house, we're loud.'

They went beyond the privet hedge, banged loudly on the door before opening it with Saul's key. They left the white van, prominently parked, hazard lights flashing, doors open like an ambulance, nothing to hide.

'Bit niffy,' Sarah sang out.

They would find what Saul had left because they knew where it was and he had told them. They went in blazing, as if they really were the cleaning team, turned on the hoover, turned on the kettle in the grubby kitchen that was beginning to smell after four days. 'You've got to be the genuine thing,' Sarah had said, 'otherwise you fool no one. We really are here to fumigate this house a bit, so that's what we do, whatever else we do – so once indoors, I get on with it, you find the stuff. You've got to have respect for the role,' she said. 'You've got to become it.' She was in her element.

They felt safe to explore above the noise of machinery with all lights blaring. As long as there was that noise, anything went. They were official because they looked it. Saul had been quiet and secretive; they were the opposite.

'Right. What have you got?' Sarah yelling to Di over the sound of the machinery, rounding a corner and finding Di standing in front of a piled stack of paper, transfixed and sorting through it.

'Plenty of . . . Oh, look at this. Can't believe it.'

'Stop it, Di, whatever it is, stop looking at it, pack it up and clear out. Hear me. Just stop looking, pack it up.'

Di packed everything she could see into two cardboard boxes, sketches and drawings, sorting as she went. Toby had made it easy. The recent work from the Life Drawing classes were in one place, the older stuff on yellowing paper, in another corner, suffering a little from damp. She collected while Sarah whistled and then dumped the boxes in the back of the open van as if it was nothing.

Then they really cleaned the house, Di's recompense for stealing.

They left the desk but cleared the kitchen and scoured the bathroom. Rubbish bags with food detritus they put by the front gate in the council bags. They left an empty house with nothing to entice the mice and rats otherwise expected soon. They swept and sprayed, so that the house they had burgled smelled as sweet as artificial lavender. Di insisted on that. It seemed the least they could do.

'I love this stuff,' Sarah said, thumping the steering wheel and driving fast. 'I love doing this stuff.'

'So do I,' Di said. 'I've just robbed a house in the street where I was born. Isn't that a thing?'

'Robbery,' Sarah said, 'is a crime involving violence. Get it right. We aren't robbers. We're collecting evidence. You offload; I get the van back, right?'

*

Paper was surprisingly heavy. The laundry room was on the first floor, pleasant-smelling and dry, with a window on the world. There were two linen presses, an industrial strength washing machine, and an armchair for the laundress. Peg's favourite room, Di remembered too late. She just wanted to put the recent work somewhere very clean and warm and let the residual smell of that dark house evaporate. She took the other box up to the main room to have a better look. She was dithering, adrenalin-fuelled, climbing down, becoming more organised. So, Life class stuff, recent, in the laundry room, the other box of the older things in the main room, her room, to look at them there. She tipped the box over, letting the paper fall out; then put it all back. This was for Saul, not for her. He was keeping out of the way until later; Sarah was returning the van. The house felt far too empty. The old paper smelled of old man. Di opened a window, let the sharp spring breeze in. Spring was coming, summer soon.

Toby Hanks, fine artist. She could hear the voice of her Thomas, talking. *Steady on*, he was saying. *I don't feel good about this*. Neither did she.

She dragged the box to the basement, then, desperate to get out of this empty house, pushed her arms into the sleeves of a coat and went out to walk.

Early dark and the pier at its best, glinting with light, a beacon for the busy. There was only fishing off the pier, no amusements, no great beauty either, except for the string of lights that joined the lamp-posts and shelters. She almost ran towards the legs of the pier, following the tarmac cycling path that flanked the steep shingle beach where she had played and swum forever. If she got to the end of the pier, she could look back at the town; see buildings weaving away on either side, the richer, the poorer, the one-time brothels, the surviving pubs, a frontage of fascination. The pier was a place she embraced and shunned, but it never failed to give perspective.

What do I want to do? Who am I? I don't want to talk to Thomas any more, I want to talk to someone else. I want to talk to Steven. I want to know what he is to me. I plucked hair from his head and tore hair out of my own, thin crop. Off it goes, in a pack, according to online instructions. He wouldn't do it, I have. Not my brother.

Am I a collector or a thief? All I know is that at the moment, I don't know who or what I am, except that I'm ashamed of myself.

The pier was empty of fishermen, wrong time of day or year, nothing doing by way of fish and no tourists, either. Di walked to the end, remembering that this pier was supposed to be the same length as the Titanic. Which meant, if you got to the end, and walked round the platform surrounding the empty caff, when the wind howled and the sea groaned, you could dream of romantic, heroic suicide, and an end to all confusions? Or you could look at the view, and say, *Not yet, I want to live.* Make a decision, anyway; jump now, and let the tide carry you for seven miles. Or stay still and forbid the wind to bowl you over the railings? Yes, or no; if it's yes, you want to live, then make a vow to live well and honourably. Do not ignore your father's existence, for instance – his ghost had loomed large in Dixon Avenue; perhaps that was what upset her. What was she becoming other than hard? What did you do when you knew danger was lurking? You went out and embraced it, by taking risks.

'I want to be a good thief,' Di shouted, loud enough to be heard over the sound of the sea. 'It's better than sex.'

There was a figure coming towards her on the invisible sea side of the walkway round the caff. The figure side-stepped her and came back. As slim as a reed, two inches taller, smelling sweet, booted and spurred, grasping her gently. Embracing Sarah, Di found herself crying. They were tears of frustration and confusion rather than grief.

'I entirely agree,' Sarah Fortune said, patting Di's back. 'About it being better than sex. Much more constructive use of the primal passions.'

'Tell me who you are, Sarah,' Di said. 'What are you like?'

'A catalyst,' Sarah said. 'A fellow creature in need of a drink. I suggest we go home and plot the next heist.'

'Yes.'

'After all,' Sarah said, 'there are other ways of pandering to the libido. In the absence of men, it's burglary keeps us alive. Time we looked at the bigger picture, if you'll excuse the pun, and got into serious training, such as learning the arts of disguise.'

They walked off the pier and on to the steep shingle beach, skirting the sea lit by the moon. Sarah could feel Di's intense frustration and nervous energy, didn't quite know what it was about. Di began collecting stones by the light of the moon, and then threw them into the sea in rapid succession. The movement was strong and well-practised. It seemed to Sarah that each pebble Di threw entered the sea at exactly the same spot.

'You know you're good at that,' Sarah said. 'Good at throwing stones.'

'Always was. We used to float bottles as targets and stone them. I always won. I taught myself. First select the stones, by touch. Throw each one better than the one before. When you throw into the sea, the sound of the splash is so satisfying, you want to repeat it, but I'm telling you, the sound of breaking glass is out of this world. I loved that sound, it's addictive, and that's why they chose me. What a child I was. I don't think my father needed to encourage me; I was going to do it anyway. I am so ashamed of myself,' Di said, vehemently, 'so *bloody* ashamed of this evening's work. I could drown in shame.'

Sarah said nothing, waiting for more. Di flung another, larger stone and did not wait for the sound of the splash.

'Ashamed?'

'Not because of doing it. Because of the *scale* of it.' Di was shouting, full of self-disgust. 'The pathetic, bloody scale of it. You and I, Steven and I, can do so much better than that. All those paintings,' she said, 'hidden away in dark places, waiting to be rescued. And we pose as cleaners and take stuff from a dead man's house. Too easy, it's shameful. I was far more ambitious when I was fourteen and a lot more ingenious.'

'So we should be more ambitious,' Sarah said. 'Use our combined talents for the good of art preservation. It's OK if it isn't for personal gain.'

'It wouldn't be stealing,' Di said. 'It would be more like releasing prisoners.'

'Releasing hostages. I'm sure Saul has a list of establishments for our attention,' Sarah said. 'And we both might know where to begin. I read the Winifred Doris email, thanks. Toby Hanks, Kemsdown, it all connects.'

'Does it?' Di said. 'I don't know, I just don't know.'

'You will,' Sarah said. 'You surely will.'

CHAPTER SIX

Well, I'm relieved that Di's alive again, Sarah wrote in her journal. *She needs more than one project; the exhibition, yes, the collection itself, yes, but she needs more than that. Fact is, Di needs a man who won't be just any man, but she also needs a career as a rescuer, a nurturer, and other deep waters in which to swim. An identity. Excitement, the use of skill. She needs to fill her horizons with a crowd of challenges, maybe stop thinking of her dead husband as a saint. She needs to keep her wits and her ability to sidestep, because she's still in danger. Just because Patrick loves her doesn't mean his family no longer want to destroy her. They have been denied their inheritance: if they cannot have it they would rather smash it.*

The success of the planned exhibition, and Di's higher

profile, is very likely to inflame their envious hatred. They are waiting for an opportunity.

I wish I knew either more or less than I do. I'm relieved that Steven Cockerel now communicates with me, encouraged by Di. She wants him to know everything about her. I don't quite know his agenda, but I know he wants to protect her.

And as for me? What do I want out of this? Love, fun, risk. I'd like Di and me to perfect our devious arts. It looks like Kemsdown may present an opportunity. Di needs to know more about disguise. And could we have a bit more frivolity, please?

Putting Toby Hanks' life drawing sketches in the laundry room was a bad idea.

'*If* you don't mind my saying so,' Peg said to Jones and Di in her mock parlourmaid voice, 'I think that was a pretty shitty thing to do. Saul goes in this old man's house and nicks his best paintings. Then you go in and nick the rest. I don't get it. I went to prison for less.'

Peg was stroking the ears of the dog which sat next to her on the floor of the laundry room, resting against her thigh. She had once been afraid of dogs but when Grace came to live here with her compromised digestion and occasional weirdness, a relationship developed against all her resistance. Grace made it perfectly clear that she would rather be alongside Peg than any other person on the planet and Peg was flattered. Grace was a tart, Sarah said, and Sarah should know.

'Shit thing to do, steal from a dead man, I reckon. You've got his dog, then you steal everything else. All right, he might have thought his dog was dead, but what kind of example is that? Then you dump these drawings in my laundry room and tell me "don't worry"? And what do you want me to say when the police come round?'

'We did clean the house while we were at it,' Di said.

'Makes all the difference, doesn't it?'

'I'm sorry,' Di said, genuinely remorseful. 'From now on in, if anyone asks, you can say you know nothing about it. Sorry, you're right, this shouldn't involve you in any way, shape or form. Sorry.'

Peg shrugged, disinterested in anyone else's moral confusion. She wanted her unsullied room back; she did not want Di crowding in on her space. Jones was OK: Jones often sat with the washing, and he was her ally, although not without reservation these days. He should have been furious with Sarah and Di, and especially Saul, but curiously enough, he wasn't. He was volunteering to carry the box of drawings away, signalling to Peg to keep her cool, and shushing the women out of there. He remained behind after Di had gone, intent on reassurance.

'It's not quite stealing, this time,' he said. 'Not quite theft. There's a definition of theft that says it involves the intention to "permanently deprive the owner of ownership".

Borrowing, keeping in safe custody, well, that's another matter. You can't go to prison for that.'

'Bollocks,' Peg said. 'It's nicking stuff that isn't yours whichever way you look at it.'

'Problem is,' Jones said, 'if this crazy gang didn't take old Toby's paintings, well, nothing lasts long in Dixon Avenue, not in an empty house.'

'Yeah, yeah, and if someone comes looking here who's going to believe about not "permanently depriving"? And what about us, what about *me*? I'm not going back to prison for sitting on stolen goods.'

Jones saw her point. 'Wouldn't you rather know what's going on? You're always saying you want to know.'

Peg shook her head. 'Not this time I don't,' she said. 'And I'm glad they've cancelled the painting class, too. I want nothing to do with any of this. I'm leaving this story. And so should you, Uncle Jones, you really should.'

'You might be right, girl,' Jones said. 'You might be right. I'll be back for that box in a minute. You never know,' he said, pointing, 'you might be in there. He drew you, didn't he?'

He left the door open as he always did and she slammed it behind him. Old people never finished conversations; they sidled away, leaving her sanctuary invaded. Peg was in two minds as to whether to shout, or spit on one of Saul's shirts. They knew nothing. She blew her nose on her own sleeve, and looked at it, disgusted. Then she turned to look at the box of pencil sketches, saw a folder newer than the rest, labelled LIFE CLASS. Toby's drawings. *You might be in there,* Jones had said, which meant he knew she was and while Peg did not want to look she had to and there she was, right at the top. There were several different versions of herself from the first class when she had modelled so defensively.

Toby used small A4 paper for the fast sketches. It was good paper, she could tell; creamy and thick with a surface that blurred the dark pencil lines into something soft. The fast poses captured her profile; another sketch her uncertain hands with long, artistic fingers; another, her feet which the dark pencil seemed to have elongated. Peg looked at her own hands, proud of them; she always looked after her hands. Then she found the sheets depicting her as she was for the long, twenty-minute poses, capturing the way she had stood in that first class: head turned, arms crossed, feet tapping, waiting to flee, an angry creature trying to stay still. In these drawings she was shaded and contoured and fully formed. Peg could see a furious beauty, a creature of determination, nobody's fool, with curves to die for and a great head of hair. She could have been a vintage film star, a graceful icon, a statue. On paper, she was a strong woman who could also dance and was light on her feet; she was alive: she could stand her ground or take wing. She was lovely and angry. It took her breath away.

'You do all this with lines, you know,' Peg told Grace, who sat on her feet. 'Only lines, straight lines and wavy lines, you know. That's all drawing is. Only it isn't, is it? I'd like to keep these. Show them to my kids, when I'm old, like forty. That's me, I'll say.'

Peg separated the drawings of herself, rolled them carefully and put them in the back of the linen press. 'These are mine,' she said to Grace. 'I want to keep these, are you listening to me? Am I listening to myself? OK, I'm glad I've been stolen. I'm glad I've been kept safe and these pictures of me haven't gone on a bonfire, 'cause I want to keep them. What does that make me?

She rearranged the contents of the folder to make it look as if nothing was disturbed, and then hauled the box outside the door for Jones to remove. *I'm bowing out,* Peg said to herself. *I'll be out of here, taking these as a reminder of who I am. That makes me just a little bit of a thief, because I'm not going to give these back to anyone. These are mine.*

Course, I'm not going anywhere yet. Not until after this exhibition we're going to have. They'll need me for that. I'm beautiful, I am. There'll be a party, only I wish it was somewhere else. Di does, too.

The dog looked at her, ambled to the door to be let out and sat as if on guard. When Jones removed the box down to the basement, Grace followed and was turned back.

Peg reflected that it was sad that Jones no longer

trusted her the way he had. Otherwise, she would have told him about Di's dad; about how she had seen him in a pub with old Hanks long before the Life Drawing class and about how they might have been mates. Well, if you don't ask, you don't get told, and he should have asked and she wanted out of the story. Peg did not like to tell Jones that, by now, she knew his own town better than he did.

Di watched Saul, sorting and examining paper in the full grey light of the upstairs room, listening to his frustration.

'Take them away,' she said. 'Take them down to the basement, please.'

'No dates, no signatures. I just don't know, I just don't know.'

'Go and live with them,' Di said. 'You need to spend hours with them.'

'And then what are we going to do?'

'Nothing for now,' Di said. 'Only dwell with the situation we've created, get on with other projects until we can find out who is truly entitled to own these things.'

'And then?'

'We return them.'

'Do we?'

'And in the meantime,' Sarah said, coming into the room, 'Diana and I are going to take recreation. Devote ourselves to retail therapy and learning the cosmetic arts of disguise.'

'The better to be thieves?' Saul said.

'Maybe.'

'We'll let a little time pass, shall we?' Sarah said. 'Nothing can happen until I find out about Toby Hanks and his heirs and assigns. My appointed task.'

'Let a little time pass,' Di echoed. 'Wait. Winifred Doris said to wait.'

It would only be a matter of time before an empty house in Dixon Avenue proved irresistible. A group of kids came round the back one evening, ready to explore, see what there was, running away when they saw who was there. A man with a hat over his eyes who told them to fuck off out of it. There was nothing for them to gain anyway; nothing to drink, nothing to smoke. The man prowled round the house, thinking how clumsy the previous intruders had been. However much they thought they had covered their tracks, they were not very good at it. Someone had left a cheap ring by the kitchen sink. There was a cap with traces of red hair. They did not know how thorough you had to be in the removal of fingerprints; water alone did not do it; he could see smudges on the walls. Sure, they had cleaned, but they hadn't worn gloves as he always did. Not that anyone was going to care, but if anyone did, there was plenty of DNA about. Everything important to old Toby was safe.

He thought he had better muddy the scene a bit more.

The man limped round the dead man's desk, collected all the paperwork. Then he went and piled a few of Toby's dirtiest clothes in the living room and set them alight. He doused the smouldering garments, creating thick smoke, and then put the fire out. He knew how to control a fire and dirty a room.

This was not a particularly clever way of covering tracks but then he was not always a clever man. He regretted it as soon as he had done it. He sat down, thinking that in some way, this was all turning out exactly as Toby would have wanted. His paintings were safe.

Jack Quigly, Di's father, sat still and lonely, his laughter hollow. If only his daughter had not ignored him on the cliffs when he had seen her, she could have saved herself this trouble. If only she had recognised his shouting voice when he had seen her with Edward. He had wanted to ask her for help with Toby Hanks and she had rolled away and talked into her phone, and then ran, shunning him and making him angry. *Look at me,* was what he wanted to say. *Look at me. I'm not Quig the hobo any more. And those bastards are planning to get you. Mind, I didn't want to get close to that dog. I told Toby I'd put it out of its misery, and it might have a memory of me.*

Now he supposed he could work on the house. There was a nice fireplace lurking in this room. Renovating the house wasn't much compensation for the absence of the occupant. Old Hanks had made him handsome.

His phone rang.

It was them, again. Edward and Gayle, requesting information.

Be polite, OK?

PART TWO

CHAPTER SEVEN

'It's very good of you to come out with me,' Steven said, formally, with his strange good manners that Patrick liked a lot. Steven reminded him of his grandfather, who had shaken hands on first meeting, and on departure, always pressed something into his palm. A stone, a sweet for the journey, a coin or a note. Patrick had folded his grandfather's gifts into his fist and his pocket, and only ever looked at them later. They were not always surprising but ever welcome. This man, Steven, was handing him an entrance ticket. The desire to put it in his pocket and keep it for later was almost automatic.

'So good of you,' Steven said. 'I love coming here. I usually come on my own, but it's much more fun this way. So kind of you to accompany me.'

So kind, so kind, so kind. Like he was Grandpa, appreciating his opinion. Not only was Steven offering to take him round London looking at painting stuff, he had given him the choice of what he wanted to see. They had settled on the National Portrait Gallery, which had actually been Di's suggestion, because that way, she said, you saw several centuries' worth of painting in different styles and hundreds of faces and you might pick up a few ideas. Patrick liked faces. He also wanted to see how you hung pictures of faces; he was thinking of the exhibition they were going to have and trying not to worry about it, though worried he certainly was.

Wouldn't he prefer something more modern? Steven had asked. No, thanks. And there was the particular exhibition for which Steven had bought the tickets. Portraits of servants; not lords and ladies, only servants.

Patrick's first meeting with Steven had not been auspicious. Steven was known as Daddy's friend, began visiting out of the blue two years before, trying to buy something Dad had. He didn't buy, but Dad still fawned over him. Dad and Mum didn't know that Steven was also Di's friend and while Patrick had no idea of the nature of the relationship between the two of them, he knew by instinct not to mention it. If Di said Steven was OK, he was OK and they had become unspoken conspirators. Another thing: when Steven called at his parents' apartment near the station where he got off the train, he made a point of speaking to Patrick as if he was an interesting adult. There was none of the suppressed exasperation of his father, none of the disappointment of his mama, just straightforward interest. Patrick had always been a preternaturally silent child, the better to avoid provoking his parents' impatience. He had become the quiet observer of their enmity with an unfair world, so silent they forgot he was listening and voiced opinions that perhaps should not be voiced at home. How good was this, then, to be with a grown-up man who listened and asked. Maybe the fact that his parents jumped at the chance to dump him on anyone who offered might have been a little insulting, but Patrick was beyond all that. They never seemed to see him. Today he could be more like the child who tore round Di's seaside house and knew every painting in it. Including the ones Saul had put in the basement the night before Patrick left and he had photographed along with the walls. He did not want to think of that and of how his father was obsessed with the place.

It would be at least a few weeks before he could go back, Mum said. School, and all that, the beginning of the spring term. Steven seemed to bring the sea closer, he had a fresh smell, knew the territory, he said, so they had that in common, too. This Sunday outing was a bonus, a breath of freedom. It was like being on the brink of something and wanting to dive in.

Apart from the shaking of hands, Steven did not

attempt to touch. No manly slapping him on the back, keeping his respectful distance, no invading his space. Patrick was glad of that, at first, but as they proceeded round the gallery, found he was more than content to stand close and would not have minded a hand on his shoulder. He liked the way Steven looked; he needed a friendly male figure in his life and he wasn't a stranger. Looking at paintings with another person, each adapting to the pace of the other, was nicely intimate. They strolled at the same speed, neither pretending to like what they did not, seemingly drawn to the same things.

The exhibition of pictures of servants was below stairs, rather dark and crowded, with people shuffling from one painting to the next, in tune to the words in their ears. Steven and Patrick had ignored the offer of headphones, no thanks, want to go at my own speed without all that yatter yatter, which seemed to impede the business of looking, so the two of them abandoned the prescribed order and gravitated to the least crowded exhibits. There was a preponderance of servants in livery, looking dutiful and unsmiling, as if they were modelling their uniforms on parade. There were game-keepers and splendid butlers, ghillies and shepherds, men with hounds. There was not a lot of below stairs and no one was actually painted doing the washing. Patrick had a nostalgic memory of Peg with no clothes on. Peg wasn't a servant; truth to tell, he wasn't entirely sure what a servant was. Scant knowledge of history and fact and period costume dramas his mother liked informed him that rich people had them, but no one was called a servant in his world, let alone a master. Both were slightly alien words. Houses cleaned themselves, didn't they?

'What *is* a servant?' he asked Steven.

'In this context? Good question. Skilled people employed to look after houses, livestock, all that. Lifelong dependants on their employers, hence wearing uniform. They may never do anything else or know another world. They live with the family but apart, like in attics or stables. And,' Steven said, leaning forward to examine a pink complexioned portrait of a shifty-looking butler, 'they sometimes steal the silver.'

'Is that's why he's so red in the face?'

'Could be,' Steven said.

'I don't think so,' Patrick said. 'I think he's been stealing the booze.'

Patrick could not equate any of these portraits with anyone he knew. Next, a portrait of a stalwart housekeeper, squint-eyed, severe in brown bombazine, holding a fistful of keys, nothing servile about her at all.

'She isn't a servant,' Patrick said. 'She's definitely the boss. They need her more than she needs them.'

'Lovely paintwork, though, look at the way he's got her. Face like a gravestone, wouldn't like to meet her down a dark alley at night. She'd lock you down the cellar and throw away the key.'

'She smokes cigars,' Patrick said, and found a delirious rise of giggles in his throat. Starting down in his solar plexus, gurgling up. 'She smells a bit.'

'What would you do if she came up close and said "Give us a kiss"?'

'Run away!' Patrick said, unaware that his voice came out as a shout. Everyone else around them was so reverential, shuffling about, saying sorry if they bumped into one another.

'Underneath that skirt,' Steven said, bending to Patrick's height, 'she has fur knickers. And black stockings. As well as two chickens and a squirrel.'

The giggles remained under control, just. They went on. They sidled through the crowd listening to their headphones, young Patrick head height with earnest bosoms, looking at the paintings he could see. Stopped, suddenly, not minding colliding with Steven. 'I like that,' he said.

Tiny little portrait of a servant, seen from the back, bending from the waist, sweeping the corner of a wainscoted room, with the light coming in from a window. The only portrait of someone doing something, the only natural, spontaneous sketch of activity in the whole thing. No face. *Unknown Artist*. 'Oh shit,' Steven said under his breath. Then, 'I like that, too; very much.'

Next a stylised painting of a woman wearing an enormous mob cap, bottom balanced on an invisible chair, hands linked in her lap over a pristine white apron, staring straight ahead as if straining to keep her head on her shoulders. Her small yellow hands were out of scale and she was challengingly demure.

'What's under that hat?' Steven asked.

'Sausages,' Patrick said. 'A lot of sausages!' His stomach rumbled.

'So she has,' Steven agreed. 'Just what we need.'

Later, outside in the street, Steven found himself in the company of a twirling boy dangerous to traffic. The rapid injection of bacon sandwich caused a sea change from a boy who flopped and giggled to one who was dizzy from food. They ate as if they had stolen it. No breakfast for this boy; this boy sent out without food. Talking like a drain, united in trust by shared silliness. Sausages.

'Yes, well,' Patrick said, gulping and slurping, and now rushing out the words in some kind of order, gesticulating. 'Di's having this exhibition, you know. My idea, just mine. About guilt. So you look at a painting, mainly a portrait, and say, what have you done, what are you planning to do? What have you got under your hat or up your skirt? Or down your trousers? You know, like an exhibition, of fifty paintings where you look at the face, and you guess what they are. What they're thinking.'

'Do you get given a clue? Like the descriptions by the side?'

Patrick nodded so hard his hair flew. Glorious hair he

had, too long and dirty blond. 'Clue is, they're all guilty about something. We're going to write a caption for each one, which says what we think they're thinking, like someone says, I wish I hadn't stolen that ring I'm wearing. I wish I didn't have a stolen chicken up my skirt.'

He collapsed into giggles again, hoovering up milk-shake, waving his hands and scattering stuff over the table without noticing.

'Or sausages up my hat. OK, more than that. You put a label on them. Thief, witness, drug smuggler. And it makes a person look, and say, not to me, you aren't. To me you're something else.'

Steven suddenly loved this boy with the words tumbling out of him. Loved him, loved watching him, crazy little sugar-drunk.

'Brilliant. Look for the guilt. Guess what it is. Tell you what,' Steven said. 'Don't know if you noticed how people looking at paintings always look at the description first? Or listen on the earphones, to something that'll tell them something about it? They read before they look. I do, anyway.'

'Yup,' Patrick was nodding again. 'I don't much, but people do. So I reckon the captions had better be brief. Like, I'm nasty. Doesn't matter who made me.'

The high blood sugar faded from peak. He inhaled his drink; put it down with a thud.

'It's going to be brilliant,' he said, slumping back in his

chair, 's'long as Mum and Dad don't ruin it, 'cause they're going to know and they're going to try and put a bomb under it.'

'How so? Why'd they do that? How will they know when it happens?'

'It's going to be public, isn't it? Course they'll know and they'll want to spoil it. They already know about it because I had to tell Mum. I wanted to tell her. They hate Di,' Patrick muttered, closing his face into utter appreciation of the last of the milkshake. Regret was expressed, subject closed. Time to change it for now, so Steven did.

'When I go to an exhibition like the one where we just went,' Steven said, 'I play this little game, like I think, which of these do I want to take home? There's always a favourite, the one you want to kidnap. Put under your coat. Maybe two or three, but always one first.'

'The bestest one,' Patrick said, eyes alight with understanding. 'The one that's got the mostest. Like, you love it best. Maybe because it's not the best thing, but it's the one that talks to you.'

He held his head in his hands, elbows sliding on the shiny table, considering the problem. A wise boy, Steven thought, delighted with him.

'It's that little person without a face. The one that made you say, "shit". Best thing. Best paint. Know what? That one was the best painting. More than a portrait. Wasn't a servant, was just a person moving in the light.'

'I couldn't agree more,' Steven said. 'Where did you get your eyes?'

Patrick shrugged. 'Granddad's house. I got used to looking.'

He was restless now, wanting more of the looking.

'And now,' Steven said, 'we're going to see something else. Going to stop looking up and look down. We're going to look at art you can stamp on. You can walk all over it with hobnailed boots. You can disrespect.'

Led upwards by the grand, sweeping staircase that rose from the front entrance of the National Gallery, it was easy to miss what lay beneath the visitor's feet on the landings flanking the staircase. The flight of steps made the visitor look up and look forward, rather than down. Who would be interested in the floor when being propelled uphill to the contemplation of the sublime as well as the museum shop. The man who made these mosaic floors, Steven was explaining, had a sense of humour, and he once said too much art is above people's heads. In all senses. Well, this isn't. These mosaic floors aren't ancient Greek, and they aren't supposed to be taken seriously. They're done for laughs and surprises. They're jokes, portraits of people, they embody being English. Look, here's Winston Churchill, standing on the white cliffs of Dover, looking like a bulldog, encircled by the word 'Defiance'. He faces a swastika-shaped monster and orders him away. Then there was a man using an enormous, almost comical electric drill, playing it like an instrument to symbolise Engineering. Farming was summed up by a woman scrubbing a pig, Music by a clarinet and a shell with a sheet of music. Football was a square design, with two men tackling each other and grinning. In the sequence in the east vestibule, about The Pleasures of Life, Patrick loved 'Christmas pudding', a pudding aflame with brandy, and one vignette called Mud Pie, showing three mud pies, one with a flower stuck in the top. In the west vestibule, he particularly liked a coal miner at work, and a spinning, clumsy acrobat, symbolising Theatre.

Thirty-six individual mosaics in all, the colours intense, the expressions as clear as oil paint, the playfulness paramount. And you walked over them without seeing them at all. Patrick was enchanted. He lay down on the floor to feel the texture, see how it was done. He sat on the mud pies. Nobody minded that. He felt he had discovered a secret no one else knew. Steven tangoed over the floor, danced from right to left. Then he did a little tap dance routine, making a noise with his leather-soled shoes. 'I like coming here,' he said, ending with a flourish. 'You can stamp on heads without doing any damage. It's cathartic.'

The man who did these, Steven said, was a Russian. Did them over forty-eight years, including the war. He was a bit of a scoundrel and people loved him. Funny how you don't get loved for being good, Patrick said, but you get forgiven everything if you're funny.

'Is that how you cope?' Steven said as they walked into spring sunshine, ready to begin the day all over again.

Patrick considered that. 'I draw funny pictures of people, and they like them. I drew you, you know. Can I do it again?'

So Steven sat on the steps in Trafalgar Square in the spring sunshine, trying to look nonchalant, only a little embarrassed and then proud of the company. Don't look at me, Patrick said, look away. Ten minutes was all it took for Patrick to produce a sketch of Steven dancing, a nice likeness, even without much of his face. Patrick tore it out of his sketchbook and handed it to Steven. 'Thank you for the mud pies,' he said. 'I'm going to make mosaics out of sea pebbles. I'll make seagulls and dogs and faces out of stones.'

'I like this version of me,' Steven said, looking at the sketch, rolling it up carefully and swiftly and putting it into his top pocket, bowing at the artist. *So do I*, Patrick said, but didn't say it out loud. 'You're as daft as Grandpa,' was what he said.

'Ah, yes,' Steven said. 'I'd love to know more about him. I met him, you know, I must have been about the same age as you, taken to tea. Now, do we do more art or more food? Teatime, isn't it, and you can have enough of art. Could you possibly have the time for tea?'

The formal manners were back along with the silliness. He was like the Mad Hatter in *Alice in Wonderland*. Patrick looked at his watch. Four hours had passed, feeling like minutes.

'She said, be home by four – Mum said.'

'Ah,' Steven said. 'Three stops on the Piccadilly line. We can walk up to Green Park and stare at people on the way. Flower stall there, buy your mother some nice flowers, don't you think? Shall I take you all the way home?'

'No.'

A short distance, flowers purchased, in the form of a small bunch of imported anemones, in vibrant colours. Patrick had his Oyster card in his pocket, sophisticated Londoner he was, could go anywhere and had done for years.

'Goodbye, goodbye, goodbye!'

Having said it three times, Patrick ducked inside the entrance to the Underground, waited a few seconds and came back out. Steven was standing there, facing away, seemed to be blowing his nose before starting to move. Patrick knew he was going to follow him home. He knew it was not far to where Steven lived, Pall Mall, junction with Jermyn Street, something like that. A breeze, allowing for the crowds and Steven walking slowly. Turn left, turn right, hang back at the traffic lights, turn down a wide street full of big buildings. Yes. Steven lived in a big building that had once been a bank, Mum said. That would be it; the place where he stopped and Patrick moved to sprint past him. But instead of pressing the keypad by the door,

Steven turned round and surveyed the street in either direction, the way he did to make sure he was not over-looked, so they practically bumped into one another, Patrick still carrying the flowers. Steven put his arms in the air, as if surrendering, acting surprised, although Patrick had the feeling he wasn't, not quite.

'Hello, my dear friend,' Steven said, with the same formality with which they'd begun the day. 'Are you lost? What brings you here?'

'I just wanted to know where you lived,' Patrick mumbled. 'Wanted to see it.'

'Good,' Steven said, gently. 'So now you know that you can come here any time. But I can't let you in today, much as I'd like to.'

'Why not?'

'Because I'll be suspected of being a paedophile. I'm afraid men of my age can't ask little men of your age into their houses. When your mother and father say yes, that's another matter.'

Patrick nodded, accepting. 'Yes, I know. Just like they said about Grandpa. I didn't want to come in, I just wanted to tell you something. About Mum and Dad. So you can tell Di. Cos I can't, I really can't.'

The words became stuttered, the lights changed and the traffic roared. Steven bent closer to listen.

'Just tell Di that they talk to her father. They talk to him quite a lot, ever since they knew there might be an exhibition. He's a bad man. So it can't be good. Can it? Think they might be trying to get Di's dad to bugger up the basement.'

Steven nodded in a way Patrick found infinitely reassuring. There was nothing condescending about it. He was right; Steven understood.

'Taken on board,' he said. 'Give me your hand.'

Patrick extended the hand not carrying the flowers, and felt Steven fold two notes into it. He put his fist into his pocket immediately, the way he had with Grandpa. Then Steven was hailing a taxi.

'That's enough to get you home,' he said. 'And get you back here, any time, if ever you're in trouble. I wrote my number on a note, OK? And we'll fix another outing to a place I'd really like you to see. All right?'

Steven opened the door of the taxi and ushered Patrick in. 'Please take this prince home,' he said to the driver. 'He's delivering gold bullion and sausages and is a very important person.'

To Patrick, he was mouthing, *see you soon*. And Patrick laughed half the way home because someone else knew what it was like to be him.

Steven keyed his way into the great front door of the ex-bank building, ran up the stairs to his penthouse flat, stabbed at another keypad that had replaced the lock with a code changed every few days, flung himself inside and went towards the window. *Too much art is above people's heads.* From here, he could only look down.

I'd kill for that boy, as much as I would kill for Diana Porteous. What is the matter with me? What's happened to me? The fact that there was a painting by Toby Hanks in that exhibition this afternoon becomes completely irrelevant. I am losing the objectivity that made me rich.

He consulted the email messages of the day, never took his iPad out of doors, not even at weekends, one thing at a time. Yes, he knew about Di's father, she had told him, although only a potted history, so he did not know enough. He knew so much and so little. He emailed Sarah Fortune, a not quite precise message: *Hope you don't mind, but can you tell me about Di's dad? A dicky bird tells me that he is in communication with Patrick's father. I need to know more so that I can find out why.*

Only six o'clock on a Sunday afternoon. He wanted to roar and stamp on heads.

Another email from the Kemsdown museum. He had enquired about another painting, backing up the email with a letter. The response was brusque to the point of rudeness. No, he could not see the small painting, by appointment or otherwise. Store under refurbishment. *Due to cutbacks, we no longer have a curator.*

Seagulls flew over his penthouse, howling at the dusk, and he wished he was closer to the sea.

CHAPTER EIGHT

Picture. *A view of the beach from ground level.*

Let a little time pass, to give perspective to the view, Sarah said. There is a huge virtue in doing nothing for a while, except researching what we know.

Dear Steven, Sarah wrote. *You asked me to let you know about Di's dad. This is what I've picked up from several sources: Jones, Di, a little from Peg, and I've scanned you a drawing Patrick did of him, two years ago. This is all with Di's permission, of course: she says she'd rather I tried to explain him to you than she did. She says she thinks my overview of information received might present a more accurate, objective picture, since I'm the only one round here who's never met him.*

So here is a report on Mr Quigly, aka Quig. Ex-army, a tad brutal, married Di's mother a few years after you were born. Widowed when Di was ten, gets her hooked up with a gang of thieves and when later she goes to prison, he is out of the country, as he often is. Quig graduated from being rat catcher/ poacher to being a gifted and innovative disposer of bodies, both animal and human. His services as unofficial gravedigger are much in demand. He is currently absent, or maybe not. Has a variety of places in which he might stay, although may live in France. So not an assassin, a dealer in carrion, living in an alternative world.

His greatest infamy was attempting to kill the dog, our Grace. Leaving an animal for dead on Di's doorstep was abominable, but according to Jones it was actually meant as a kind of gift. Jones despises him for being a wastrel and a hobo as much as anything else. No respect for property, Jones says; never owned a thing, which is a sin in Jones's eyes. Jones respects property.

Quig is a threat to the enterprise, not because he is physically dangerous, but because of what he knows. He's intimately acquainted with the geography of this house, and probably some of the less fortunate events here. There is a lot of subversive information he could give to Di's enemies. Maybe Edward and Gayle are using him to dig the dirt? Di doesn't know why he would be in liaison with G and E, except to exert some power over her, keep alive the threat. (Note: Quig was in communication with them before they came to raid the house, but there is NO evidence that he assisted them in any way.) The last time Di spoke to him, he kept saying he only wanted to help. It may well be true, but his idea of help may not be constructive.

I can't comment on events that took place before my delightful acquaintance with this ménage. My guess would be that Quig, a man despised and rejected, knows that he has lost his daughter, and in some way, wants her back, or at the least, some influence. Worst case scenario is that all of them might imagine that Di's early demise would be financially rewarding, though Di says that money was never really Quig's motivation. I know she thinks of him often and have to say, it's my belief that it's unlikely she'll form another meaningful relationship with another man until she has reconciled her relationship with him.

Peg will only say he has lovely hair, she washed it once. More than that she won't say. If anyone has seen Quig in the vicinity, it would be her.

Overlong and possibly not very helpful. I know Di's spoken to you separately about other issues. Incidentally, I love her very much, more than a real sister. I might even kill for her. Just as long as you know.

I know she has a plan for us to come to London soon. Di wants the three of us to meet. She suggests the Foundling Museum, a favourite place where Thomas Porteous took her in the past. I look forward to it. We are going for a little therapy first.

Meantime, on with our separate researches.

*

Di walked Grace on the beach. That could never be Peg's task; Peg did not really do walks on beaches, even on blissful days like this, when the old shingle was full of treasures. *There is no life whatsoever on a shingle beach*, Di had read. No marine life, no plant life, no animal life, no life at all. The movement of the stones eradicate any such possibility. You want life, crabs and worms and insects, go play on a sandy beach. To Di, the stones had a life of their own, along with the pieces of shells, the feathers caught amongst them, but mostly the stones. Flint grey, mottled white, shades of tan, dead black, stones to be painted upon, thrown, collected, not one of them the same weight or shape as the next, each as unique as a fingerprint.

Patrick had told her on the phone about the mosaic he planned to make, along the lines of those on the floor of the National Gallery. *You know*, he said, *we can make an underfoot seagull of unreal proportions to be constructed by the cycle path and all made out of the flatter beach pebbles.* He had already designed it and it was to be about three feet long. So, would she please start collecting stones by colour, so he would have material ready before he arrived? Of course she would. Look, there was one of the purest white, going into the pocket of her coat. And what shall we do when we've built this giant bird out of grey stones and yellow and pink? *We'll keep it for a bit, admire it, and then we'll put it all back on the beach where it belongs.*

'And what do we do with the paintings in the basement?' Di asked Grace. 'How do we get them back to where they belong?'

Saul is trying to establish whether they really were painted by our Toby Hanks, by comparing them with the sketches we took from his house – a futile exercise, I think. Steven researches what the Kemsdown is supposed to have and it seems they are the official owners of our stolen paintings. He is sure the Director will block any direct approach and is very dodgy. Not that could we make a direct approach, anyway, offering to return the paintings, because how would we explain our possession of them? Most importantly, he has also found out that there is no curator, let alone one known as Winifred Doris. I have written to WD, but she does not reply. I am relying on information from someone who does not appear to exist and I believe every word of it.

'What next, Grace?'

Grace was used to being asked questions to which no response was required except her presence. She still loved the beach on which she had once run wild and abandoned, although there was a fragment of memory that told her she did not want to be here alone and she was always looking back. What she had not forgotten was the constant, indiscriminate starving that led her to wolf down anything resembling food, however indigestible. She would eat dead chips and the paper in which they came, with predictable results, so not always an easy animal, then, but a sweet one.

She was subject to odd behaviour at the moment, pawing at the basement door, making a fuss of Saul, sniffing the air around him. Di looked down; ah, there they were, a series of pinkish pebbles, waiting collection. Grace rolled back, dribbling at the mouth and looking guilty.

The walking of graceful Grace was also the making of friendships, a part of belonging, nodding and smiling and pausing. Dog walkers seemed to know the names of the animals, rather than the owners, though sometimes they knew both. ''Lo, Di, how's her gracious?' 'Hello, Spam, my you've grown.' Grace had spearheaded Di's gradual reintroduction into one stratum of society in this town: the people with dogs who walked this far stretch of the lifeless, lively shingle, and seemed to be her kind. 'I'm sorry for your loss,' one said, shyly, referring to her widowhood. Also gossip today. 'Heard about that fire in Dixon Avenue? I don't know what the world's coming to.' 'Look at that dog of yours, she was running wild, wasn't she? Lucky to have you. Sorry about your loss.' Things said, sympathy expressed, two years after the event. Di had felt she was disliked, but learned here, on the beach, that it was not so. This was where she would begin to advertise the exhibition, the opening up of her house. This was where she had learned to decrease her isolation. This was where her new reputation was built, not as a gold-digging widow, but a nice young woman with a rescue dog.

'What are the priorities?' she asked Grace, who did not listen and was suddenly anxious to get home – oh dear, what had she eaten? The making of the exhibition, the opening of the collection, which could surely not take place as long as there were illegitimate paintings on the premises. So, the glorious paintings of T. Hanks must go home. The first step in that direction, Sarah said, was to get inside the place and find out what was going on, and what the Director was hiding. No point to return them to a place where they would not be safe. The first approach, Sarah said, must be by stealth, in order to establish a means of returning the paintings, if appropriate, which must also be done by stealth. And then there was a young man flying by on a bicycle and Di followed him with her eyes. What was it like to make love to a young man? Was it better or worse than the considerate, imaginative love of an old man, like Thomas, and was it better than teenage rape? No, not rape, as such; she had always been too willing to please to refuse. 'Don't know anything about men,' she told Grace, 'but I dream of them all the time.' *And I don't want a lot of them, just the one. I am never going to play the field. Sarah knows this.*

There was a figure on the edge of the sea who might have been her father, but when Di looked again, it clearly was not. *And now,* she thought, *my father, back on the scene: I can feel it and Steven tells me Edward and Gayle are in contact with him. My father knows more about me than most, although he does not know me at all. I don't think he hates me; I think he loves me in his way and that is so much worse. This is something I have to sort, because my conscience is not clear in his regard, and I cannot bear to live with a cloudy conscience. He really did not need to encourage me to be a thief when I was a child; perhaps he tried to stop me, I don't know. I think of my father, and think of young men; can you figure it out, Grace? And what do we have for breakfast? What on earth have you eaten already?*

Breakfast, dinner, tea, a house always ready with food. Her mother could cook, and she could, too. Her father hated good food and pretty things, poor man. He hated what he could not understand, smashed up stuff his wife collected. He shot birds out of the sky because they outwitted him and because he could. He had never had the pleasure of owning anything.

Less of this and get home. Saul has been busy over the last week. All those sketches laid out on the cellar floor, so that he could make comparisons between the fully fledged paintings of TH and the sketches. She had little faith in the process. The door remained closed at all times. Di went in round the back; Peg was mistress of the front. Things must change. *And Sarah and I, well we have a plan. Got to go to Kemsdown and meet this Winifred Doris who is not replying to emails and may not exist. Meantime, learn disguise. We are going to learn to make up our faces, so that we look and feel completely different, and we are going to meet Steven and make the plan. No hurry, no pressure. Sarah is also doing research into the possible heirs and assigns of Toby Hanks. Each to our own skills.*

Saul was in the kitchen when she got home. He was a man who ate like a sparrow and was enormously fussy about what he consumed. There were two entrances into his grand cellar: one, he said, for the public, accessed from the back road, and one from the kitchen, via a big door with wooden stairs twisting down. The sprung door from kitchen and snug was usually shut. Saul was at the door from the kitchen, left open on to his own territory, fussing about, fretting.

'A man rang the bell,' he said, 'asking to do a market survey. Terribly nice, badge and everything, but I told him to go away, I'm afraid.'

'Next time, let him in,' Di said. 'I know you don't like it, but this has got to become an open house.'

'Is there food?' he said. 'Only I need food. A bit of smoked salmon, and an egg?'

He was worse than a child, sometimes, and Di thought it was as well she loved him. Scrambled egg, the way he liked, with chives for colour, a bit of fish, and his skin went pink.

'I keep looking at them,' Saul said. 'Got them all laid out on the floor, two dozen sketches, laid out in rows underneath the TH paintings, trying to see where he was coming from, trying to make comparisons, looking for clues. Not getting anywhere.'

'Maybe nowhere to go. Maybe not the same man. Maybe someone with the same name.'

'Don't know. The sketches I've got are no way preliminary sketches for what T. Hanks subsequently did. They may be from long before, mostly long after. I did so hope for evidence. And, some of the recent Life sketches are missing, pity; there was one of me I'd rather like to have. Are you sure you got them all? I'm just beginning to get clues. Get back to it soon. Thank you for the food. Is coffee a possibility?'

'I took every sketch that was there, and yes to coffee.'

He watched her rise, and knew why Thomas had loved her, graceless, sandy little creature she was, even in her new clothes. Neither noticed the dog, Grace, slipping down the steep stairs from the kitchen.

'There must be something to link the old work and the new,' Saul said, fiercely. 'There must be, has to be. I'm nearly there, nearly there. Can see a line that equates to another line, another thought. These sketches must marry up. But they don't, yet.'

'You can't force them to be what they aren't.'

'We've got to go and see what there is in the Kemsdown place.'

'Who's we?'

'Sarah and you.'

'Yes, I know. We're planning, and it's better you don't know.'

'Yes, it is.'

'Go for a walk, Saul. Look at the sky. You spend too much time looking down.'

Yes, Sarah and she were going to go to Kemsdown, and it was going to be planned with Steven, not Saul. Steven knew what was there; Saul did not. Sarah was pursuing enquiries with the local solicitor, deputed by law to investigate any possible inheritors of the T. Hanks estate. That was where she was today, each using their separate attributes.

'I suppose I should go out,' Saul said. 'Look at the sky, I mean. It might be good for me, all that fresh air. Maybe I shall see more in these things if I walk away from them. The problem about these newer sketches is that none of them suggests an ounce of the merit or the themes in the finished paintings. I shall walk. Now.'

When Saul walked, it was a route march, a walk with a purpose of getting him up to a high point to march down again, go sideways, traverse a certain distance, come back without looking at anything at all but refreshed all the same. He never came back with stones or feathers in his pocket. If he looked at the sky, he would prefer it painted in oil.

*

Sarah sat across the desk from the old-fashioned solicitor in his shabby room at the top of the high street, opposite the hairdresser where Peg was working out a traineeship. He was as dated as his room, discreet and law-abiding beyond his young middle age. The soul of probity, obedience to rules and slightly pompous.

'Thank you for the appointment,' she said. 'I made it because I'm concerned about Toby Hanks, the artist, recently deceased.'

'Are you family?'

'No, no, but I was acquainted with him. And now I hear his house was damaged and he's still in the mortuary. I wanted to know what happens next.'

'Ah. If you aren't a member of his family, I can't talk to you. Sorry.'

A rules-are-rules man, until there was a glimmer of recognition.

'I know he died of natural causes, bad heart, recently treated by doctor, so no inquest pending.'

'Correct.'

'Can't you tell me anything more about him?' Sarah asked, lamely, a little taken aback by his officiousness. 'Can't you regard me as a fellow solicitor and a kind of cousin?'

'At risk of repetition, unless you're a blood relation, no.'

'What if I were to say,' Sarah said, 'that I might be in possession of something that belonged to him?'

'That would present me with some difficulty,' he said.

One of those; oh dear.

He had been staring at her suspiciously and then, suddenly, he clapped his hands to his now-beaming face.

'It's you!' he said. 'Of course! Of course it's you. How wonderful to meet you. I didn't recognise you with your clothes on. How do you do? Life Drawing class,' he said. 'I'm an occasional student. Not on the day Toby pegged it, though. Best model, bloody marvellous. Are you coming back?'

'I hope so, when they start again. Are we so radically different without our clothes?' she said, laughing.

'No,' he said. 'I'd have recognised you instantly, only for the fact you're wearing make-up today, ha ha. And now, Ms Fortune, since you've modelled for me and our mutual, deceased acquaintance, I think I can regard you as a member of the family. Fraternity, whatever you call it. What do you want to know?'

'Were you a friend?'

He shook his head. 'Not as such, only nodding acquaintance at the class. I go when I can, enthusiastic amateur me; he was always there. Perhaps why he brought me this piece of paper, last year after he came out of hospital. Asked me to keep it and sort things out when the time came. I said yes, but he'd have to make a proper will, all he gave me was a short letter saying what he wanted to happen. He's effectively intestate, if you know what I mean. Did you say you were a solicitor?'

'Once,' Sarah said.

'Good Lord. Figure like yours and a legal brain. I could do with some help. The letter names a beneficiary without giving an address, and it sort of appoints someone to take charge, again no address. And there's a sort of bequest for a memorial stone to a dog. He had a dog he loved. If there's one thing I dread in a will, it's a bequest to an animal, alive or dead.'

'May I see it? This invalid will?'

He hesitated.

Di was in the upstairs room, Saul out on his therapeutic walk, when she heard the echo of an animal, howling, as distant a sound as a faraway ambulance alarm that did not stop or fade away. It sounded like a piece of machinery gone wrong, nothing more, until it repeated itself and demanded investigation. She expected the sound to diminish as she walked downstairs into the kitchen, but instead it was more prevalent and clearly came from the cellar. Grace, the dog who was not allowed down there, was howling through the open door. Di went down.

The sketches that Saul had laid out on the floor in serried rows, the better to inspect, were saturated, torn and chewed. The prevalent smell was animal, rather than Saul's discreetly perfumed human. Grace had sicked up whatever she had eaten on the beach either before or after she had scratched all the paper she had assembled into a torn pile, turning it into a scrambled heap on which to lie and mourn, like a widow on some funeral pyre too damp to light. Grace could produce copious amounts of fluid. She had even rearranged her destruction to make a bed of it, scattered it, reassembled it with her great big feet and surprisingly effective claws, and she stood in the midst of it, baying. Her great brown head was turned towards Di, while her feet were still rooted in rubble. She was pawing away at old smells, as if trying to find the familiar source. She stopped when she saw Di, hung her head in what might have been shame, a picture of red-eyed misery. Something clicked; of course, Grace had once been Toby Hanks' devoted dog.

'Come along, old girl,' Di said. 'Let's get you cleaned up. Sorry about your loss, I didn't realise. Come along now, out of here. Let's bathe those poor eyes.'

It was one of the moments in time when she realised that she was not a pure collector like Saul, because the animal mattered far more than the ruined sketches. The dog with the missing memory had found a residue of it. Something, if not someone, had loved Toby Hanks.

'You need a makeover, Grace. There, there, I'm sorry. He didn't mean to leave you. Peg'll be home soon. There, there.'

The dog mattered more than the sketches it had destroyed. Was she perhaps reacting instinctively to the sketches on the floor, intimately handled by an old owner, full of his scent? Looking for him? Memory, where are you? There had been no reaction at all to the paintings lined up against the brick wall, no marking of territory there. The framed paintings had been lightly handled by TH, perhaps not recently so, while the work on paper, especially the older stuff, would bear the scent of Toby's blood, sweat and tears.

She cradled the dog's head in her lap and bathed its inflamed eyes. 'There, there girl, it's all about smell, isn't it? You just needed to be close enough to smell.' Did it follow that TH the artist left no smell on the older, finished oil paintings? No scent to compare with that left on paper over years?

She should have asked her father why he had tried to kill the dog, instead of simply despising him. Had he been asked to do it?

Later that evening, when Sarah had come in and out, and Saul had been inadequately consoled and the dog was with Peg and Di was realising how relatively powerless she was, even in command of a room as grand as this, she got the email from Winifred Doris.

Hello, dear Mrs Porteous!
　　Sorry I haven't been replying. Been unwell, got weak heart, like half my family, nothing terminal, ha ha!

So nice of you to take an interest and I have so much to do. We have another ghastly exhibition upstairs. The store becomes ever more vulnerable and the Director impossible, so I've moved to stage two, which is another way of answering queries he's blocked!!! (He never locks his computer because he doesn't know how and can't ask.) I am beginning to send the paintings to those who enquire about them. No rush, then. Time is useful stuff, wish I'd used mine more productively, hope you use yours for laughter. Don't for God's sake devote your life to looking after anyone else, especially an Artist. Paintings never leave you, artists do.

Remember how to get in at the back. Don't ask nicely, it won't work. You'll have to trick him.

Must go. Work to do with my little pliers and knife . . . No one here but me and the damn dolls.

I swear they come alive at night. I do.

Steven, in his eyrie, read the email and continued his research. On Google Earth, he could see the contours of the building. Nothing for it but to go there, to that not very significant town with a Cathedral Close and an urban sprawl. He would be surreptitious, survey the scene to check if the information given by the elusive Winifred was accurate.

Meantime, in a mere thirty-six hours, he would see his

beloved, who as he well knew was not his sister. They would all meet at the Foundling Museum, which was also the place he had suggested to Patrick for their next outing. It was a place where you learned things about yourself as well as looking. He had always loved it.

A package arrived by post in the afternoon, addressed to Steven Coke in childish handwriting.

The contents consisted of a watercolour painting, frameless and backed with cardboard.

He wanted to keep it.

CHAPTER NINE

> Picture. *Interior with Two Women.*
>
> *Looks a little sinister. A woman sitting in a canvas chair, utterly relaxed and sleepy, reading and wearing a skull cap, while another woman stands behind her, smoothing green unguent into her face and neck. Circa 1920s.*

The capable hands of the woman behind could be intent on throttling. Why should one woman stroke the throat of another?

In fact, a domestic portrait of that era, of two women having a beauty session in the kitchen, entitled The Facepack. *One was the artist's wife; the other a student who went on to pioneer medical illustration. An oil sketch infinitely capable of misinterpretation. Perfect for the exhibition.*

Early in the morning, Di finished her notes on this newly acquired painting, because it was strangely relevant to the first part of the day ahead in London. Yes, it was perfect for the exhibition, but the exhibition was not something she wanted to think about, purely because of the basement.

Disguise, Sarah said, disguise, disguise, disguise. Dear Di, I've realised the importance of make-up when it comes to making an impression, especially a wrong one. Today is the day we go to meet Steven. I have insisted on this frivolity beforehand because it's important in its own way and I need it even if you think you don't. Don't alter the plan.

Sarah meant the specific plan made the week before, pursuant to her greater, ongoing plan, which was to get Di out of her house and out of her town as often as possible. To make her face the world with greater confidence in better clothes and more effective disguises; make her a person not easily dismissed by the art sharks and bureaucrats with whom she might one day have to deal if the collection was going to go public. Sarah was not worried about Di's perceptions of the wheelers and dealers in Saul's world, because Di was thoroughly underwhelmed by pomp, circumstance and had no doubt about her equal status when it came to knowledge. She was at home with people twice her age and not easily intimidated. No, Di would make her own judgements and had her own sophistications. What concerned Sarah was not what Di thought of *them*, at first and second glance, but what *they* thought of her. She could be too easily dismissed. Di did not make immediate impact. Beauty was power. Good looks demanded second looks. Sarah wanted Di to use everything she'd got. Progress had been made in the matter of clothes so that Di now loved fabric and colour, cashmere and silk, things that felt good against a salty skin. She knew her own shape and would never wear anything that might stop her from running. Once acquired, she wore a new item indiscriminately, silk trousers at breakfast, cashmere on the beach, merino wool to pick blackberries. There was no best and second best, they were simply clothes that she wore without any sense of occasion so that it was no wonder the dog walkers were so often delighted and charmed. She could ring the changes with clothes, distract or disguise. So far so good. It was her face that gave her away because it was such a naked face, a far too open book with a limited repertoire. She needed disguise for her eyes.

Here they were, London for the day, to plot and plan with a serious purpose, beginning in the salon of Sarah's choice, ready to experiment with the cosmetic arts. You are here to learn how to change your face, Sarah said, either to make you feel like a different person or reinforce your identity. Something to make you more recognisable, or less, she said. Give you another layer. I wonder what Madame de Belleroche, or anyone scheduled for a portrait, did to themselves before they were painted? If it was me, I'd rush for my own paintbox long before the artist arrived, so that I could show myself in my best colours before I was examined. That's all I'm asking of you, dearest Di. Give it a go. See if cosmetics can widen your choices and make you a better actress.

How sweet this was, letting someone paint your face. Di didn't know where they were. She could have been on another planet, and she could remember the picture she had shown Sarah, of the two women doing self-improvement in a twenties' kitchen that somehow made this all right because it had always been done from the ancient Greeks to the present and for now, she was ready to be altered. A makeover in order to become more courageous; looking forward to seeing Steven and wondering if it would make any difference to him.

She was asked by a young man how she wanted to look. He turned her face to the light and stroked her cheekbones as if he was cleaning a picture with devotion rather than duty. He loved his task like any genuine art restorer and that comparison was also comforting. 'Wonderful skin you have. What do you want to be?'

'I've no idea.'

'I see,' he said, and he did.

There was a soothing process of stroking with cool cleansers on cotton wool; then we moisturise, then we build a preliminary layer, then the lightest of foundation. Then we concentrate on the eyes: *you have extraordinary eyes.* As long as she thought of him as an artist in his own right, Di was content. She was halfway interested in the process while more than halfway dozing, watching him pick his precision instruments and talking to himself, now this goes with that, and that goes with that colour. A realisation that, yes, this might make a difference; thinking of herself bathing the face of Grace the daft dog, who had seemed to be weeping and was left this morning with her wagging tail and her revealing eyes. Di's hair had been pinned up; she liked it that way; she was suddenly mature. The smallest dusting of blusher; an extra sweep of mascara so that the eyes seemed to widen with every stroke, making her liken herself to a portrait. She was thinking that she could look like a Gainsborough aristocrat or a Gothic heroine. This artist could make her look like Cleopatra. The possibilities were endless. She could look like someone she did not know at all.

'Do I know this person?' Sarah said. 'Keep the hair pinned up, do you think?'

'*Comme ça?*' the Artist said, twirling around the chair, clipping Di's hair into a knot, with sandy tendrils escaping. 'Such cheekbones, hey.'

'Yes, I know this person,' Di said, looking in the mirror,

wishing she had listened to the Artist's explanations of what he was doing. What a wide, kissable mouth she had, feeling only a little silly when she pouted and made an 'O' at her own reflection. Hers was a petite face with eyes mirroring a mysterious soul. Or not; simply the same person subtly enhanced and looking particularly well. She fluttered her eyelashes, admiring their length and feeling them heavy. *This is me; another version of me, one I would like people to know.*

Sarah going through the same process in the next chair was another matter. Sarah knew what she wanted and she was using herself as an example of how the cosmetic makeover could not only make the subject emerge the same but better, like Di, but radically different and in Di's eyes, worse. Sarah's face looked hard and dangerous with black-lined eyes and crimson mouth. She was theatrical and dramatic and while Di's hair was restrained, Sarah's was an angry cloud that seemed to influence even the way she walked.

'In my other life,' Sarah was explaining as they glided out of the salon, 'I used to go for a makeover before important meetings. Added-on aggression sometimes helps.'

'You want to scare Steven? Is that it?'

Steven was making a list of what he wanted this meeting to achieve and wished it was not a habit. This was not business: there did not have to be a target and a quantifiable result. It was mainly for the pleasure of it, surely. No, it wasn't; it was more than that and he looked forward to it intensely. He was perfectly well aware that he would be under scrutiny from Sarah Fortune and welcomed the challenge of that. There were things to report, matters to discuss, plans to make for what was becoming a team. Meeting at the Foundling Museum was killing several birds with a single stone, Sarah said.

The Foundling Hospital, London's first official orphanage, sponsored by Handel and Hogarth, was a haven of peaceful rooms devoted to children, music and paintings. Elgar held fashionable concerts to raise money; Hogarth donated paintings and persuaded others to do the same, so that the great and the good flooded into these elegant rooms, while out the back, single women left the babies who would otherwise starve. Thomas Porteous had loved it and had once lived nearby. It was, in a way, a blueprint of what he wanted to achieve. It was a place to remind a person of their privileges in all ways, Sarah said, and also a place where you could see the best practice of hanging paintings in a grand, domestic space. Steven approved too. Patrick would love this; he already knew he was bringing Patrick here next and the appointment had been made to show him what was effectively the first public art gallery of English painting. It reinforced the Thomas Porteous vision of educating and inspiring children and adults alike by introducing them to another world through paintings, art and philanthropy combined. The place breathed warmth and efficiency, giving remembrance of thousands of dead children and thousands more alive. All of them had more than one thing on the agenda. Steven had at least three.

I trust Sarah absolutely, Di had said to him. *I want you to like one another.* He was not going to try to impress; no point in that: they had already trusted by email. When he saw them coming into the foyer of this both grand and humble place where he had been for the preceding hour, his jaw dropped. There was a moment when he did not recognise Di at all; only a moment but enough to note that she was looking so radiant it made his heart contract. He kissed her lightly on the cheek and inhaled her unfamiliar perfume smell. Sarah thrust forward her hand with its scarlet nails, making Steven recoil for the second before she laughed.

'I know,' she said. 'Ghastly, isn't it? It isn't me, I was trying to make a point.'

'Which was?'

'That she's a chameleon,' Di said. 'A snake with different skins. And she would like your advice on which skin to wear when she and I go and raid the Kemsdown Museum. Which you are going to tell us how to do. Because you know more than we do. And you've been there.'

'A flying surreptitious reconnaissance only. Enough to discover no Director, no Winifred Doris, no budget and lousy security because someone is trying to run it into the ground. Shall we look around first? See how the pictures here are best exhibited and at the same time remind ourselves of how lucky we are? Thank you for sending me the images. And then I can bring you up to speed. I have news and possible plans.'

Again, that strange, almost comforting formality that Patrick had noted, a sort of shyness that Sarah approved.

They wandered round, Di enchanted again by the paintings in the ground floor rooms, featuring touching scenes of christenings and reunions, events occurring in the room where they hung. The surviving foundlings had limited choices; apprenticeships at ten, domestic service for girls, military for the boys, the narratives veering from the awful, to the triumphant, to the others who simply survived better than they might have done. The place did not counsel perfection either in terms of its paintings or its achievements, but it was the opposite of despair. It stopped Di in her tracks, as it had before, filled her with gratitude and a touch of guilt. At least she had had a father who fed and clothed her and that was better than having none.

At the end of the pier on this blustery spring day, Saul resembled an orphan. It was a surprise for Jones to see him sitting with his back to the wall of the caff, regarding the sea with indifference and looking shocked and weary. He had been OK, yesterday, even if the damn dog had all but ruined that mouldy pile of sketches that Jones had since removed. *No merit in them anyway,* Saul said, as if that was all that mattered. Merit? What did that mean? Saul was more sad than angry. He was a bit of a shadow of his former self, although immaculately dressed in a way that didn't accord with his slump. Normally, he stood and walked like a dancer with a spine as straight as a cane. Had to be something wrong with him coming down the pier like this because he loathed it and the wind messed with his hair. He was so different from the fishermen here, he might as well have been painted pink or purple and was the only person in a hundred yards with polished leather shoes.

'So what gives?' Jones said, sitting down heavily beside him.

'Oh, hello,' Saul said distantly, touching the stubby fingers Jones held loosely in his lap looking as if they were simply waiting to be useful. Jones felt moved by the touch. Saul was a member of an alien species and Jones was unaccountably fond of him as he would be of a deluded child or the lost, errant teenagers he had so often rescued. Saul was a poof, but he was brave in his way, didn't tell tales and was good at clearing up. There was a lot to respect and that was all that counted. They looked out to sea where the storm clouds were gathering as a reminder of how bad it could be long after winter had passed and how much more dangerous the summer storms were.

'Tell me something,' Jones said. 'I was going to bow out

of this story, but now I can't, so I need to know. Why are those two silly bitches planning to go to this big old art gallery at the other end of the county and first have to go to London to plot it?'

'They're going to research the returning of stolen goods, namely the twelve paintings in the basement by an unknown master and I'm not sure if I can bear it, any more than I'm sure if this Kemsdown place is where they should be. Just because the labels say they belong there, doesn't mean they do. And,' Saul said, 'more to the point, I have been proved to be incompetent and worse than that, my dear, it seems that I have been *exposed*. Discovered. Both as a useless researcher, an incompetent custodian and a thief.'

'You what? A thief?'

'A thief. Someone knows I took the paintings from Toby Hanks' place. Today, when I was coming down here for another view of the world, a boy ran after me, and said, I think you've dropped something. He handed me this little scroll, like a relay runner passing on a baton, so you take it automatically, and maybe say, thank you very much. Like someone handing you a bar of chocolate to promote the brand. Until you open it up and there you are. Your very own self. Look, here I am. Straight out of the portrait class, via Toby Hanks' house.'

It was a rolled-up sketch, oil on paper, from the penultimate class, dated not signed. Oil portraits in the morning session. A biro scrawl on the back. *I saw you.* The unfurled sketch showed Saul's inquisitive face in half profile, with a fine nose, a knowing eye and a hectic skin. The man to the minute, Jones thought, although not kindly depicted and not the man he knew because he was looking a bit cruel and calculating. Well, Saul was a bit eccentric, but he wasn't bad, though the sketch did make you think twice. Jones didn't know quite what to say, until, looking out to sea, the penny dropped. It was all about the trespassing and thieving.

'Ah,' Jones said. 'Someone sending you a message, right? Where do you think this picture came from?'

'From Toby Hanks' house, I guess.'

'Not from our house?'

'No. It was there with the sketches when I went in the night Toby died. I saw it, on top. I only took the twelve framed paintings. Di and Sarah went back later and took all the existing sketches that were there, I'm sure of it. This one wasn't among them.'

'And brought them into the laundry room, big mistake,' Jones added, continuing the story. 'And in the morning, young Peg took out a few, I know she did. But not this one of you, it isn't among those there, I looked. Never was. She only took the ones of her. So, someone removed this from Toby's house between times. And now sends it to you. Fuck. I'm guessing someone saw you go in, and wants you to know he saw.'

Saul nodded agreement, miserably. He was on the verge of weeping and Jones hated to see it.

'Think on, Saul. If someone was there in between, took out a likeness of you and gets it delivered, he's delivering you evidence. Evidence that could link you with the theft. He's saying, I know you were there, I want you to know, but I'm giving you back the evidence. I'm not going to use it. I'm giving it back.'

He stood up and paced around, watching the gathering clouds that Saul ignored.

'Whoever this is, Saul my man, I'm not sure he's your enemy. Otherwise he'd be holding on to this, not sending it back.'

Quig, he was thinking, *fucking Quig*. This had all the hallmarks of Quig. It was far too subtle for feckless, artless, owning-nothing Quig, but still Jones thought of him.

'My enemies are legion,' Saul said. 'And by the looks of this, the worst of them is me.'

'Hang on again,' Jones said, getting up and sitting back down. 'If this person saw you, mightn't he also have seen Di and Sarah? Might have kept on watching? Shit, Saul, I don't ever want Di going to prison again.'

'And I,' said Saul, 'have no wish for these superb paintings to go back to prison either. Although it does seem imperative that they should be removed.'

'Are you angry with the dog?'

Their hands touched again and there was the ghost of a smile on Saul's face.

'Of course not,' he said. 'How could I be? The dog is a

thing of beauty. Wasn't the dog's fault. The dog had the right judgement. I was going to congratulate it.'

'Peg's already doing that,' Jones said. 'Who do we tell?'

'For the time being, dear Jones, absolutely no one. Especially not the women.'

'Just sit tight, and wait on them, right?'

'What is clear,' Steven was saying, 'is that the twelve paintings you have in the basement are technically the property of the Kemsdown. They were privately donated and according to the records, they're still there. Director says they're out on loan, being restored, but that's probably a lie. You may have the mirror images of the Kemsdown paintings, or more likely, these paintings were stolen, either by your Toby Hanks, or someone who passed them on to him. Nobody knows until someone goes and looks. As for Winifred Doris, well, I don't know. I've looked up employees of the museum. No one with those initials, even. I guess someone has to go and find her, even if she has no real existence.'

'She does in the imagination, whether she works at the museum or not,' Sarah said. 'She writes from an email address which isn't the museum's, could be any old internet caff. But one Winifred Doris is named in Toby Hanks' makeshift, invalid will. Here's a part of it I was allowed to see. *To Winifred Doris. Have the lot back. Jack Quigly will fix it. I appoint J. Quigly to fix it for me. He knows how and he's been good to me.'*

'Thank you,' Steven said. 'What did you have to do for this interesting information?'

Sarah raised her enhanced eyebrows, fluttered her lashes in a parody of flirting.

'And why is my father, Jack Quigly, in contact with Edward and Gayle, Patrick's parents?' Di said, ignoring the mention of his name in the context of Toby Hanks. *He's been good to me.* What did that mean?

'That's been a little more difficult to find out,' Steven said, 'without compromising Patrick and letting on how well I know you. I had to be talking about Patrick and his well-being. The most I could discover from Edward over a pint was that they worry about Patrick's welfare when he stays with his nameless step-grandmother, i.e. you. They fear the house is not safe. Something about the basement not being safe after building works. So they contacted a neighbour of yours, Edward said. Just to keep an eye on things. I had to leave it there. Couldn't be too specific or curious.'

'So my father watches, reports on the building works,' Di said without bitterness. 'And has been watching and waiting to help. He was born in Dixon Avenue, always went back there. Perhaps not surprising he knew Toby Hanks. It might not be a new thing, him talking to Edward. Just might be the first time Patrick heard it. I've deliberately avoided any knowledge of my father's whereabouts, anything about him. I shouldn't have, I owe him more than that. Poor Patrick, having to be an informer. Thank you for hearing him.'

'I love Patrick,' Steven said, simply. 'We have a plan to come here, next week. Do you think he'll like it?'

'Yes, I think he will.'

Di felt the handle of her coffee cup in the light, airy café of the Foundling Museum where women left children in the hope of their survival, not as an act of abandonment but of desperation. Next door was Coram Fields with its farm, where adults could not go unless accompanied by a child. Thomas had taken his children there; Patrick would come here with Steven. It was a place where you consulted your own past luck and she was so incredibly lucky that she had not been an orphan left at the door. When she had come back to the old schoolhouse by the sea after prison, she too had been a lucky foundling.

'Ah,' said Sarah. 'So Quig lived in Dixon Avenue and may haunt it still. Makes me wonder what else your dear father knows. Did he see us? Might he have seen Saul?'

'It doesn't matter,' Di said, fiercely. 'It really doesn't matter. Don't pursue this with Edward, Steven, don't blow the cover. It doesn't matter. Having a watcher like my father on the case presents another complication. Not a threat, only a complication. I don't believe he wants to harm me. I think he wants attention and he may want to help. I shouldn't have ignored him. He's a brute, but he gave me a childhood after all. And he might have been asked to kill the dog out of mercy.'

She was with two people she loved, discussing others she loved, in a place she loved. She had never worn a uniform; she was not an orphan; she was a person with an identity and big, wide open eyes, and in this moment, Di felt incredibly, recklessly happy.

'Main thing is the exhibition in the autumn. It's Patrick's brainchild. It's about doing something of which to be proud. Ignoring nameless threats. Not waiting for storms. It's about the house and the collection becoming a place a bit like *this*,' she said, waving her arms towards the paintings on the walls. 'The house could become an institution like *this*. Where young lives could be made better by looking at beautiful things.'

Her smile was so wide that Sarah laughed. Such a contrast to their lips, Di's smiling rose pink and her own, threatening crimson, the difference between the persuasive and the aggressive. *Let Di take charge*, Sarah thought. *She's better at stealing stuff than me. I thought I was good at this, but I'm not. Left my peaked cap in Toby Hanks' place, didn't I? I left traces behind that someone burned. Don't think of it; think of the next thing. I wonder if he watched?*

'Kemsdown, next stop. When?' Sarah said loudly, punching the air.

'Wait a minute,' Steven was saying. 'This has got to be planned. Listen to me. I've been there, I've reconnoitred,

I've been refused an appointment, but I've inspected. Appalling security out the back where the workers go to smoke. They've got a common exit with the council offices. I've got photos. And . . . '

'And we know from Winifred Doris that the Director is a vain man, susceptible to women,' Sarah said, raising her pencilled brows. 'Computer illiterate. About my age, I think. I like them lonely. I wrote to him, got an entry. So you see, Steven, there already is a plan.'

'I'm beginning to think that we shouldn't rely on any information supplied by Winifred Doris. Because whoever she is, she's not who she says she is. But her geographical information is certainly sound.'

He was formal again, a stuffed-up, youngish man. Sarah feared he lacked imagination. He could not possibly be Di's brother.

'We go anyway,' Sarah said.

'Look at the website again,' Steven said. 'Look out for the automated models. They seem to be the only things of the original art collection on display. You'll love the current exhibitions, not a painting to be seen. Why don't I come with you?'

'No, definitely not,' Sarah said. 'Women's work. We infiltrate, we make up a story, we flatter and deceive. We'll be much better at that than you. That Director would never have anything to do with you.'

That was something Steven had to concede, while

thinking that Sarah might be over-elaborating because she wanted an adventure. Well, what harm in that?

He thought of the package he had received the day before. It had contained an original little watercolour he had asked about, neatly removed from a frame. It bothered him that he did not want to mention it, at least not until he knew how it had occurred. Someone had sent it from Kemsdown and he wanted to keep it.

Sarah was in full flood.

'We have maps, we have directions, a goal. First off, all we have to do is find out what is in this store this Director man wants no one to see. No danger in that. Surely not. We do it on our own,' Sarah said.

'And I have to find Winifred Doris,' Di said. 'Of course she exists.'

No danger, surely not.

Only a fantasist and a vain man, no danger at all.

Here's the plan, Sarah said.

Let's go. Soon.

CHAPTER TEN

The day dawned. The rain eased and the sun came out. There was a jet moving over the blue sky, leaving a white trail that was more beautiful than anything in the room.

'Where was I, Madame de Belleroche?' Di asked, addressing the portrait that faced her desk. Madame had always been free with advice.

'My dear child,' Madame B said. 'You were acknowledging the virtues of disguise, but you look the same to me. Put me wherever you want, as long as I'm seen in daylight.'

And I, Di said to herself, *sometimes think that I would like to get paintings out of this house rather than bring any more in. Sometimes I relish the sight of an empty wall, almost as much as I dislike the idea of consigning anything to the basement. Madame B would not want to go there.*

'Di is taking me on an expedition,' Sarah told her list-less brother on the phone. 'We have to do it. I have different motives to hers, to be sure, but I do not have it in me to have only one motive at a time. I have been a lawyer, a peacemaker, a bit of a tart, insofar as I am perfectly con-tent to sleep with the enemy and talk into his ear if it helps. I have gained the attention of this Director; he is looking forward to seeing me. I need to practise the subterfuge that I was once good at before I lost the knack. This is playing with sparklers rather than fire.

'So off we go to Kemsdown, this small, cathedral town where treasures by Toby Hanks have been taken from the Gallery store. Someone has to get into the store referred to by Winifred Doris, whoever she isn't and however silent she is. We have to look out for the mechanical models used for advertising in case they have any significance, so Steven says, simply because Winifred Doris mentioned them and she never mentions anything by accident, and we have to tell him every detail of our plan.'

'And your plan is?' Saul asked. 'Let me guess. You either seduce or intimidate the Director, while Di infiltrates the premises, right? That would be your style. I'm not sure I want to know.'

Sarah drove the hired four-wheel drive with verve. Her dress for today was full grey trousers, gripped at the ankle over her petite heeled boots and a military-style jacket. Finished with large antique earrings, it was combat style with glamour. She fluffed up her voluminous hair. 'Right,' she said. 'Here we are. We've come to admire innovation.'

'Don't forget Winifred Doris,' Di said, fingering the camera round her neck and hoisting her capacious canvas bag over her shoulder. 'Don't overdo it.' Her clothes were dull and her eyes wore their cosmetic disguise, making for a pale and sulky effect.

There was an imposing flight of wide stone stairs leading into the Victorian buildings shared by the town hall, and the museum and gallery. There were five floors and the Kemsdown Museum and Art Gallery had the upper three with their storage facility on the level in between. They had a map of the floors and a plan, of sorts and some useful googled images as well as Steven's survey, all such a game. The gallery's disgraceful security loophole was the fire door that opened on to the car park at the rear of the building, an exit shared with the council offices accessed by back stairs and unused by anyone except by the smokers, who kept it unlocked for ease of egress into their secret corner. They checked this out first. Winifred Doris had been right; her information was still sound. Security for the gallery was almost non-existent because no one cared.

Basically, Sarah would command the Director's attention, and Di would explore. In the event of disasters, neither would attempt to rescue the other. They were each on their own, phones silent, to liaise at a nearby hotel, later.

There was a small, empty reception desk and the place was deserted. Next to the reception desk, there were two almost child-sized automated toys, of the kind that might have stood outside a shop luring a punter to enter. There was a seated negro, dressed in red, who would raise his hat if someone put a penny in his mouth. Next to that was a dog that would wag its tail for the insertion of a coin in the ear. The models looked as if they were guarding the place. They were sweet, on the one hand; garish pieces of social history on the other.

Early for their appointment, they detoured into the first gallery room to the left of the desk, entering a dark space, with a single white light in the centre of the floor. The large windows were blanked to the light by blue muslin tacked to the walls, so that it was like going into a blue cave and felt cold. They stood around the light, which resembled a traffic cone, and stared at empty walls. The light glowed dimly; then as they watched became brighter before dimming again. Then it blinked out and as soon as they were adjusted to darkness, proceeded to glow afresh. The whole sequence took a minute and palled quickly. They tiptoed out towards gallery two. A bare room of the same generous size was bathed in red. The large windows had been papered over, also in red, allowing a little roseate light to filter through into the gloom. There was a single large canvas on one wall with a series of faint, intertwining question marks embedded into the grey surface. In the gloom, Di was just about able to read the three paragraphs of explanation printed on a notice near the entrance, a reminder that we should always question whatever information we received. Di could hear her Thomas talking: *If the subject of a painting could be dealt with in words, there would be no need to paint it.*

There was some distant sound which reminded Sarah of a loud lavatory flush. In the corridor, again looking like a guardian, was another of the models, this time a hideous old lady made of metal dressed in black, wearing a mob cap. For the insertion of a coin into her shoulder, she would raise the teacup from the saucer held in her lap, sip her tea and put it down again.

'Ah,' Sarah said, looking into the red room. 'I think we have a concept. A challenging concept.' She turned to Di. 'Remember the roles. I told Mr Cloake that we were an independent film company, doing a pilot study for a film about how to bring excitement into museums for the European market. He found time to see me.'

'And I'm a researcher,' Di whispered. 'I ask dumb questions and look for camera angles. You're glamorous and persuasive, and I'm uncooperative and irritating.'

They moved into the third gallery, smaller, dimly lit and bare and more like a room in a big house, highly lit and relatively bare. One more of the shop models, looking like a chimney sweep, faced away towards a video installation on the wall opposite showing a set of hobnailed feet proceeding over a desert floor towards them, getting bigger and bigger until they could see the pores of the white skin and the laces of the boots. Di noted a small door at the far end of this room, marked PRIVATE. That was the way to the store.

'What's it about?' Di whined.

'Exploitation?' Sarah said, loudly. 'Obvious. Big white legs, desert landscape.'

'Exactly,' said a voice from behind. Sarah turned her full beam upon him.

'Marvellous,' she said, in a rich, breathy voice that Di could never mimic. An image of Steven flashed up. *This man will respond better to a woman.* He was already responding. Sarah raised her glasses, touched the linen-clad arm of the Director and looked into his eyes from her cosmetically enhanced own.

'Mr Cloake, I presume. How *very* nice to meet you. *Wonderful* use of space.'

'Where are the paintings,' Di said in a petulant voice, tugging Sarah's sleeve. 'Only I thought we were going to see paintings, I thought we were doing paintings. Haven't got the right camera. *You* said . . . '

'Do forgive my assistant,' Sarah purred, gazing at the Director while taking him in. Too soon in the year for the crushed linen look and his eyes, in purple-rimmed glasses, were level with her chin and seemed to vary their myopic concentration from her mouth to her bosom. She had a slight inclination to pat his head, while her inner eye recorded: *intense, tries too hard, profoundly insecure and actually on the brink of tears. Find the right language. This is absolutely my kind of man. Frightened, wanting a friend.*

'Marvellous innovation,' she said. Key word. 'I'm Mrs Wisegarten. And this is my assistant, Kelly.' She leaned towards him, confidentially. 'Who is not having a good day.'

They raised their eyebrows in mutual recognition of staff problems. He put both his hands over hers in an exaggerated handshake, a man who wanted immediate intimacy. His palms were warm and his smile was wide and anxious. Here was a man in trouble; definitely Sarah's kind of man.

'Such a pleasure,' he said. 'Would you like to come into my office, Mrs Wisegarten? Perhaps we could discuss the *concept* of what you have in mind?'

They swept away, leaving Di with her bag in an empty gallery. She wandered back and saw the incongruous model of the waitress, sitting with the cup of tea in her aproned lap, found a penny in the saucer that she inserted into the slot on her shoulder. The dummy raised her cup and drank her tea and then went back to being still and grinning, advertising her fifties café.

Di was angry at the waste of space and found herself disliking the Director intensely, not only for being the bully of Winifred Doris. At the moment she disliked him most of all for blocking in the windows, so there was no view of the sky. Oh Lord, how it could come alive if there were paintings on the walls, looking as if they belonged. What was it Winifred had said? *This place will die without paintings?* How could he do that and deny natural light? What was the concept behind the three rooms she had seen? *Define concept. Product of the faculty of conception: an idea of a class of objects, a general notion, a theme, a design.* A bit of a meaningless word. *Conceptualise; form a concept or idea (of).* Concept of what? Did it mean you could throw together a series of objects or light effects, stand back and look at the results and then tell the world what it was supposed to mean? Do you have the concept in advance of your construction, and work towards it, or is the concept something which simply emerges by accident?

She walked back through the rooms, stood in the red light, then in the fluctuating light zone, increasingly furious and bamboozled. The lights went off and the lights went on. Perhaps it really was an intricate design, a play on the emotions; maybe it was just random. Challenging? A two-minute wonder, with the subversive effect of making the viewing participant feel utterly foolish for not getting it, and even more idiotic for saying so. It was as if these rooms of concepts and explanations were sticking up two fingers to their audience. *You don't get it, you're thick. I, the Artist, have exclusive vision.* Not at all like the artist who had applied her mascara; he had a purpose. Art had to be deadly mysterious, preferably humourless, beyond the reach of the ordinary spectator. *Maybe,* she thought, *I just like oil paint, pencil, stones and the use of skill. I hate this Director for blocking out the light, but I do love these rooms, I really love these rooms. How light and wonderful they could be, with pictures on the walls and the sound of laughter. These rooms need me. They need the sort of exhibition that would bring them alive. He's turned these potentially light-filled rooms into dungeons. This Director needs me. Perhaps this man is merely powerless to revive this place.*

Di prowled. The reception desk remained empty in the late afternoon and the blanketed rooms remained deserted. There was nothing to welcome anyone in; no one was beating a path to the door of the Kemsdown Gallery. She did not know where Sarah had gone above stairs though everything was going to plan, such as it was, being that Sarah should enter into a flattering conspiracy with Mr Director and leave her, Di, to look and locate the store and maybe identify Winifred Doris. She was distracted by liking the gallery rooms and seeing how they were dying alive. Di was having a debate with herself and feeling three years old. *Look,* she was saying to herself, *a Curator/Director has to experiment, bring in the new etc, nothing stands still. But do you therefore have to exclude the old? Treat people like idiots? I am not an idiot: Thomas taught me I was not,* *and although self-doubt is my second nature, I sense fraud.* This gallery owned fine works, which would reach out to the public viewer, would seek to include them and enlighten them about where they lived, how their forebears lived. Could delight, inform, and encourage them to laugh. *Their* plan, formed by Di and Sarah over several bottles of wine plus Sarah's enthusiasm for subterfuge, suddenly seemed over-optimistic, elaborate and a little silly. There was a greater plan, suddenly hinting itself and taking shape, to make these rooms work. Di wanted to rip down the dark-coloured material obscuring the windows.

She moved across the rooms. There was the map in her head and she had rehearsed the way. First, the fire exit, used by the smokers whose working hours had ended for today. Sarah had jammed it slightly open with a polythene bag, so that it looked closed. Now she went back to that small door in the last gallery, marked PRIVATE, that led the way to the store between floors where she could smell paintings and the silent Winifred Doris beckoned. The door opened to an uprising set of steps, which surprised her; she had somehow expected descent rather than ascent. She thought of the map; the other access somewhere else; a lift. Now she was climbing between one floor and the next, entering a long corridor, into a room lit from an opaque window that granted good enough light. Paintings of various sizes were stacked against walls, haphazardly;

there was the remnants of a structure in the centre of the room, possibly the hanging mechanism to which WD had referred in her letters. This was the store, just light enough. Winifred Doris had described it accurately. *Where are you, Winifred?*

Di noticed a single shoe on the floor in the corridor with the other shoe left in front of the first painting she examined. Then there was an abandoned scarf left over the chair looking like the detritus of an individual woman. She looked at the paintings surrounding the structure, not touching at first. Someone had tried to put this mess into order, creating untidy pyramids in the process. Canvases framed and unframed leaned against each other, languidly. A few rested against the table. Di took out her camera and put it away again. She concentrated on the paintings clinging to the last of the collapsed stacking rails. One small, unframed thing made her catch her breath. It was a free, expressionistic sketch, perhaps for a bigger landscape, showing a blue horse, munching on bluebells. It was small in its frame and so easily concealable it could slip into the side pocket of her canvas bag, easy. It was a wonderful, luminous painting, something that a child would look at and maybe want to stroke that horse. Di put it back reluctantly.

She moved carefully, losing track of time, touching carefully, getting the feel of the place, suddenly fatigued, wanted to sit down on the sole chair in the room which was

decorated by the scarf. There was a working table, no trace
of a computer, making Winifred Doris ever more of a
deceiver because she could never have sent emails from
here, any more than she had ever been a curator. Di's eyes
were heavy with the make-up that made her look sulky and
mean. Again, she consulted her mental map of the place;
two means of access to the store, the way she had come
and the other by a small lift more suitable for objects than
for large people. The lift made such a slight noise in
ascending towards her she failed to hear the Director
coming down the corridor behind, entering the room with
Sarah in his wake. It was Sarah's trilling voice that woke
and warned her.

'Ah, there you are, Kelly,' Sarah trilled in that dreadful,
breathy voice that went with her crimson mouth. 'Thought
we'd lost you. Well, well, my word.'

He, Mr Cloake, the diminutive Director with the
purple-rimmed glasses, was no longer the smiling man. He
was panting; he trembled with anger as he moved towards
Di with his hands outstretched as if he wanted to throttle
her.

'What the hell do you think you're doing in here?'

The room echoed with violence. Di could easily have
hit him, shrugged with studied insolence instead. 'Whatever,' she said. 'Bloody marvellous, this. Best installation I
ever saw. That's what this is. Concept; the redundancy of
paint and canvas. Bloody brilliant.'

Sarah flung her arms wide, embracing the scene.

'Oh, Mr Cloake,' Sarah breathed, 'you save the best till last, what a stunning tableau. Don't tell me it isn't deliberate, so well thought out. Installation art at its best. When are you planning to move it upstairs? The arrangement is fantastic! Who's the designer? Has to be you. Should be in the Tate, I'm sure I've seen something similar done with old paintings in Frankfurt. So exciting.'

Di nodded at her. *Don't overdo it.*

'Yeah,' Di said. 'Only it wasn't Frankfurt, it was Hamburg we saw it, it was called Who Needs Paint? Not as good as this. Brilliant display here. Was trying to work out how to get the impression in a photo, but you can't, can you. Not with an installation, 'cause you got to be able to walk around it. Three dimensional, this is. Has to be an action shot. I got the wrong camera.'

'Does it have a title?' Sarah asked. 'I mean this *installation*, is it yet titled? Or is it work in progress? As yet a *concept*?'

'Futility, I'd call it. Tell you what I love, that old scarf round the chair. The shoes. Offsetting something. A touch of humanity to emphasise the futility. Terrific,' Di said in her dullest voice.

The Director relaxed, slightly and incompletely. He was hesitant; Sarah's weak kind of persuadable man, but weak men were dangerous.

'She shouldn't have come in here by herself, all the

same,' Sarah said. 'I do apologise, but thank you so much for showing us. It is perfectly wonderful.'

Her hand was on his arm, again. 'I'm so sorry. She's always wandering off looking for an angle.'

He waved them in front of himself, down the corridor and up the stairs. 'No, no title yet for this installation.'

'I happen to be staying nearby,' Sarah said. 'Would you have time for an early dinner? Just myself? Kelly has friends in the neighbourhood.'

Di hated it when Sarah purred like that. The man was close to crying. 'How kind,' he said. 'How nice. Are you sure you didn't take pictures?' he added, turning on Di.

'No, I said I didn't. What lovely rooms you've got here. Shame about the windows.'

Something was wrong here: he was in a state of shock as if he was seeing something he had not seen before. He was a wreck; a man who did not want to be alone, desperate for sympathy, falling apart. Not at all like Winifred Doris said.

Sarah tossed the keys of the car to Di, who caught them. It was beyond closing time on a spring evening, getting on for seven, high time for a drink and the timing was right. Skinny, sulky Di, following them out, the two of them arm in arm, noticing how Di went back to the car and waved them away as if she was about to drive off. She already knew the way in and the way out via the fire door and was hoping it was still jammed open and there was no care-taker. Absolutely no security systems worth a candle at the back. The Director had punched the code on the front door as they left. And, if Di could not get back in through the compromised back door, she had a stone in her pocket to throw at a window because whatever happened, she had not finished and she was going to go back to that treasure house. She was going to see what else there was, and she needed to work out exactly how the Toby Hanks paintings were going to be returned and to whom? It would have to be like this, in secret, a thief returning stolen things. She had scarcely started searching, and the plan did not seem quite so far-fetched. She had the scent of Winifred Doris and she wanted to imagine these rooms with light coming in through windows.

So here am I, darkness descending in this ill-lit place, look-ing, taking apart the mess. I found the way in and I have a way out. No one knows I never really left. Sarah has that man on a lead; good. I have dismantled the installation, which was never a conscious installation, only a question of someone piling things up to hide the gaps. There are no paintings by Toby Hanks. There are a few paintings of great worth, though not in terms of cost because most are relatively obscure and some are woefully in need of restoration. There is the Eve Disher I enquired about first, and that beautiful blue horse. This store has been denuded. Somebody has plundered it of more than T. Hanks and then rearranged it. And made recent, more blatant alterations that had so shocked the Director that he was willing to be led away by a stranger with red hair and alluring make-up. He was utterly susceptible because his need was great.

So what have I done? I have walked by an old woman sitting in a chair, who on the insertion of a coin, raised a cup of tea from the saucer in her lap and appeared to drink it. Why does she stick in the mind? No alarms have sounded, yet. Until now. Winifred Doris, where are you? Did you do this? How much did you lie?

Footsteps from below; a voice, humming as someone came slowly up the stairs, too late to turn off the lights and hide or find her way to the lift and Di hesitated. As the voice grew louder and the steps closer, Di moved and knelt down behind the door where the person would enter, making herself as small as possible, feeling in her pocket for the stone she carried as her only weapon that was useless in this sort of space although comforting to touch. The woman who entered the room moved across to the desk and put her bag down on the floor, talking to herself as she did so, oblivious to the stark overhead light. Di put her head in her hands and closed her eyes, the better to listen.

'What to do, what to do next?' the woman muttered. 'She's never going to come. This place will die without an exhibition to show you all off. And you can't stay in prison for ever, my dears. I shall have to liberate you in other ways. Cut you free and send you by post, tra la la. Holes in the heart, Toby and I, holes in the heart, more ways than one. Have to cut you free.'

Di opened her eyes. She saw the back of a small, thin woman, wearing a long skirt, with her hands on hips, looking at the mess of the installation. The skirt was black; she appeared to be wearing an apron tied behind and what might have been a white surgical cap on her head. The black clothes and the white headgear gave her distinct resemblance to the model waitress upstairs who drank her tea for a penny and she was scarcely larger. How much could you tell about a person without seeing the face? This one was elderly with a stooped back, a deeply determined voice and an ability to stand still as if she was posing. Then she sighed, bent down to pick up a heavy framed painting from the floor and put it on the table, grunting with the effort.

'You're in the wrong place,' she said to it. 'Awful frame anyway, you're better off without it.'

There was the glint of a little Stanley knife, held like a dagger, raised and lowered. Di sensed some imminent and terrible act of destruction. Without thinking, she scrambled to her feet and moved towards the back of the woman, yelping rather than screaming, stumbling over a shoe. The woman's reactions were faster. She lifted the heavy painting off the desk and flung it towards Di. The corner of the frame caught her on the hip with a sharp pain, and she fell, heavily, sprawled at the feet of a tiny woman in black.

Turning off the motorway, following satnav into the town, Steven Cockerel shouted in pain.

CHAPTER ELEVEN

Steven knew he should have told them about the first package he had received from the Kemsdown and he had not done so. The watercolour in the package had been carefully removed, leaving a faint trace where the frame had been. Steven had not wanted to mention this until he knew more about it, such as: had it been sent by the Director as an opening gambit of some kind, was it for sale or was it from the elusive Winifred Doris? There was also the fact that he dearly wanted to keep it. Either way, he had thought it could wait until after Sarah and Di's foray, but then on the morning of their expedition the second package arrived as he was leaving for a crucial meeting, where he sat with the thing burning a hole in his briefcase. He was carrying it around like a piece of shocking contraband.

The thing was a tiny canvas roughly folded into a jiffy bag, paint side out and it shocked him because it had not been neatly taken off the stretcher on which the canvas had been pinned, but hacked off, losing some of the painting in the process and leaving a jagged edge. It was almost ruined in this clumsy, forceful removal. The oil was a picture of a house with a signature on the back, and it was one of the first paintings Steven had asked the Director of the Kemsdown to let him see, months ago, only to be told it was out on loan. The same painting, sent to him in person. Beware of what you wish for.

I asked to see this painting, and now, it arrives, vandalised. Concentration was difficult. The painting was a little piece of poison that told him that Di, the woman who could have been his sister and wasn't, should not be going into the Kemsdown Museum alone. He wondered where she was, what she was doing now, this minute, but then, he thought like that all the time. How long to drive? Not long. He willed the meeting to end, cursed himself for being so slow. He was fast on his feet, but oh, so slow to prioritise.

It was occurring to him, as Sarah and Di were embarking for Kemsdown, that the only possible source of the mangled canvas he had received was Winifred Doris, whoever she was. The person who was masquerading as Winifred Doris could have got his address from the letters he had sent to the Director to back up the emails. Someone had sent him what he had asked to view as a gift

180

of strange purpose. And there were the two of them, reckless Sarah, with her talent for seduction, and Di, with a stone in her pocket, exploring the place from where this gift came. What was he thinking of, leaving them to do it? There was a malevolence in this thing he was sent; a violence in the person who had brutalised it. He should have set out as soon as he had received it: he should not have delayed, should have cancelled his day. Of course there was danger: there would always be danger with those who were obsessed.

Traffic jams, motorway, all that and then there was that sudden pain in his side as he entered the town. Now he was in the empty car park at the back of the Kemsdown in his conspicuous car, looking up at a light on a mid-floor landing of the museum. He remembered the back door he had located, prompted by a Winifred Doris email, the fire door that the smokers sabotaged. It was still early evening although dark as midnight. As Steven got out of his car, his phone vibrated, shocking him so he almost dropped it while praying it was Di. It was Patrick. *Phone me any time:* that was what he had told him.

'Hello. Sorry to phone. Just checking. Is it tomorrow we're going to that museum? The Foundling thing?' Patrick's voice was high; there was traffic in the background.

'Yup, for sure, after school, good man. How are you?'

'OK. Only I can't get Di. Her phone's off and her phone's never off, she always comes back to a text.'

'Don't worry. I know where she is.'

'Just had a bad feeling, you know?'

'No worries. How's your dad?'

Patrick was gabbling and there was background noise of heavy traffic.

'Dad's not good. He knows something bad about the basement, perhaps we shouldn't have an exhibition there, but never mind. So long as someone knows where Di is. Couldn't get Peg, either, see? S'OK, now I've got you. Everything's alright as long as I know where people are. See you tomorrow. Bye.'

The call ended before Steven could ask Patrick where he was. His heart thudded along with his conscience, knowing he was never in the right place at the right time. Didn't matter how rich you were, or where you lived, it was always thus. He had a vision of Patrick standing in the busy road outside his flat in London, responding to an invitation: *you can come here, any time*. And that he, Steven, was letting him down, because he should not have made such an unconditional promise to a boy who would take it literally and he wanted to be there alongside Patrick who must be desperately worried to have phoned at all. Instead he was here, approaching a fire door, more than an hour's drive away, because he could not bear to be anywhere else. Let the door be open: there was no contingency plan. He could not throw a stone and break a window. He did not even know why he was so certain that Di was in there, except for the fact that he knew today was the day and he knew the outline of the plan. He also knew that someone who came from here was capable of slitting a canvas with a knife and it followed that the same person would have no inhibition about pushing a blade into skin. No danger, eh? Just a game, Sarah's adventure.

The door was not so much open as imperfectly closed. Steven went from the dark into the dark, glad of his own innate sense of direction and his ease with big public buildings. He did, after all, live above a disused bank. He found the door at the end of the gallery, dimly lit with security lights not connected to any alarm. Budgetary constraints, he guessed, and who would want to steal empty rooms with mission statements and raw materials of no value? If this Director was inept, he was also being constrained. He crept up the stairs to the storeroom. As he drew closer, he could hear the sound of someone crying; ragged, dreadful weeping.

'Oh do get up, you silly girl,' the woman had said to Di when Di had sprawled at her feet. 'You can't be that badly hurt. Or did you biff your head? Is that it? Or are you just lying still as the line of least resistance? You needn't worry, you know. I'm not going to hurt you any more. If I'd known you weren't the Director, I'd never have thrown the thing. You should have said hello. Then I would have known.'

Di was following the line of least resistance, lying still, slightly dazed, with a pain in her hip and a lump on her chin and a smarting in her left wrist from a broken fall, the pain made better by an acute sense of the ridiculous. She got up slowly from the floor and dusted herself down, surveying the woman, now sitting in a chair, while the woman looked back at her in turn for a full minute of silence.

'Are you Winifred Doris?' Di said.

The woman smiled. Seated at the table, she was remarkably small, unthreatening and sweetly ugly.

'My code name,' she said, conspiratorially, almost whispering, although there was no need. 'Think of me as Dotty. Which I am, but at least I'm aware of it. Most of the time. A woman with a mission. Though it does seem to have got complicated.'

She broke into a laugh that was less pleasant than her smile.

'Fact is,' she said, 'when I worked here as a volunteer – as I did for a number of years – I could stay here all night if I wanted. I'd just have to sit on a little chair with a cup of tea and no one would notice me. They'd go home and I'd have this lovely place all to myself. Do you understand?'

'No.'

'Stupid, stupid, stupid. How disappointing. When you

finally arrive, way too late, you don't get it, even after all the clues.'

Silence seemed wisest. They regarded each other in mutual incomprehension. The woman shook her head, took off her cap and ran her head through a thick head of white hair.

'I'd wheel her away behind a door,' the woman said. 'And sit in her place in her clothes, just as I still do, with my tea in my lap, ready to raise the cup. I became indistinguishable from the museum's favourite mascot. Her name is Winifred Doris. He, the Director, never even noticed. Never worked out how I broke in at night after I was barred. I didn't break in; I crept in and didn't leave, I just took up my pose. I used to be my brother's model, you see. I have the ability to remain remarkably still. I can freeze myself. Much easier now I can use the fire door. I suppose you're Diana Porteous? You took your time.'

'Your real name?' Di asked.

'Tabitha Hanks, brother of Toby. We both signed as TH. My darling, darling brother, who was a great, great painter. Exhibited here, because I made him do it, oh, such a success, you wouldn't believe. And then, all the paintings went back to this room, never shown again, like all the rest. He moved away, down to your part of the country, bitter and twisted. Don't know why. He was a fool, a great big fool, and I was his model for the sequence he painted for here. All about spaces, rooms, what you can see from behind. Daylight, he loved the daylight. No one was ever going to show them here, so I came in and got them. One by one, I got them, and one by one, I sent them off in the post, so he'd have them. Better than being ignored here. But I don't know what he wanted. I loved him so much and he simply ceased to communicate. He wanted to get away from me. Holes in the heart, us two. Both of us. Damaged goods. Loved him to bits. Like twins. I am him and he is me.'

She turned her pale blue eyes on Di.

'He knew about Thomas Porteous. He tried to sell him something, but Porteous wouldn't buy. He told me long ago, before he stopped writing, three years ago. I remembered the name, although I'd forgotten it, until you made that enquiry. Was why I wrote to you. Wanted maybe to get in touch with that bad brother of mine who hadn't been in touch with me since then and sent my letters back. He'd never let me help him.'

'You knew where he lived. Why not just go and find him?'

'And risk rejection?' Tabitha Hanks shook her head. 'Besides, I don't travel well. Bad heart, you see. And I couldn't have borne to see him with some woman. Couldn't have stood it if he sent me away.'

Tabitha's voice was sinking to a murmur and she seemed to lose focus. Di snapped the fingers of her right hand and raised her voice. The left arm seemed not to belong to her. This was only the beginning.

'Have you taken other things out of here, Tabitha?'

'Yes of course, it's become my duty. At least another dozen, safe at home. Oh, my darling Toby, why did you hate me?'

'Tabitha, what's your task for this evening?'

'This evening?' Tabitha/Winifred brightened up, as if Di had asked an interesting question. 'Well!' she said, whispering. 'After a little break, I'm on to stage three of the mission. I've been hacking into the Director's computer all year, so I know who asks to see what. He never secures it because he doesn't know how and he's too proud to ask. So I can always find out who's interested in the pictures he keeps locked up in prison, poor things. To be fair, he's short on resources. So, lately, I decided that when someone nice-sounding asked about a picture, and he fobbed them off, I'd send the picture to the person who expressed an interest. That way the picture would be free. But with my arthritis, I can't get them out of the frames, so I have to cut them out. Must get on.'

She was muttering again, forgetting Di was there. She also seemed to have forgotten the painting she had thrown and went to the installation pile for another. 'Ah, here you are,' she said, picking out the blue horse in its ornate frame that Di had so admired. Tabitha took it to the table, banging it down roughly. Then she produced the wicked-looking Stanley knife, and held it delicately like a surgeon with trembling hands, considering the first insertion.

'You can't do that,' Di said.

'Yes I can. I can do what I like. This is my home, this lovely place is my home and you can't stop me. Things have to go to people who want them. I'm doing my duty. These paintings won't mind a little pain if it gets them out of prison.'

'Your brother!' Di shouted. 'Your beloved brother, Toby Hanks.'

The hand paused.

'What about him? I rescued his work and he doesn't love me.'

'He's dead,' Di said. 'He died, recently. He's dead. People are looking for you.'

'You lie.'

The hand holding the knife trembled.

'No, it's true. He died in painting class. His heart went when he was painting.'

Tabitha put her left hand, palm upwards, down on the table, very slowly. She lifted her right hand with the Stanley knife and drew it across her left wrist, making a deep, deliberate incision. Then she began to wail.

Steven heard it as he came up the stairs, the sounds of wailing and screaming and things falling over. A single voice crying, not Di's, someone else. There was blood in the hair of the small old woman he could only see from behind and blood on Di's hands. Two small women of different ages, wrestling, Di a head taller, facing away so that he could not see her face although he could see the contorted expression of the other until they moved. The room was disordered. Di's hands were on the old woman's shoulders, trying to push her down; the wailing woman was twisting, pummelling Di's chest and screaming at her, *give me the knife*. It was a ghostly, ghastly scene of hysteria, coloured with blood. The Stanley knife was on the floor.

Di looked up at Steven and her eyes widened. He acted instinctively, moved quickly and pinioned the old woman round the waist, pulling her away, with her feet kicking, holding on to her for dear life, bending, murmuring into her ear, *there, there*. She went on struggling, and went out mouthing words and then the screaming stuttered to a stop.

'Careful, Steven,' Di said. 'This is Tabitha Hanks, sister of Toby Hanks, otherwise known as Winifred Doris. She has a heart condition like her brother and I've just told her he's dead.'

Her delivery was crisp and objective, almost cold. There was blood on her face; he did not know from where. The body he held slumped; the voice whimpered. *Toby*, she said, *Toby*. Her arms flopped. Steven released his grasp, turned her towards him and took her into a gentler

189

embrace, rocking her, lifting her, not a big man himself, but huge to this small, grieving creature to whom he responded almost as he might to a poorly animal, murmuring and stroking her hair. Pity first, consequences another time. She changed: she accepted the embrace, put her hands around his waist, let her cradle him, sighing against his chest, let him fold her into himself as she collapsed against him. 'There, there,' he said. 'There, there, it's alright.'

'Toby,' she said. 'Toby.'

'I'm not Toby,' he said, gently. 'I'm Toby's friend.'

She stayed as she was, cradled, the whimpering slowing down to a series of sighs.

'Will you take me home, Toby?' she said.

'Of course,' he said into her ear. 'I can carry you. We'll both take you. Won't we? Don't want that stupid Director to find us here, do we?'

It was somehow the right thing to say. Tabitha/Winifred giggled. 'Where's home?' Steven asked.

'Here's home,' she said, 'and it's going to die. These rooms are going to die. And it's not all the little bastard's fault, but he should have stopped it.' She seemed to drift, allowing Steven to lower her into the chair. Wet wipes, dry wipes, were produced from Di's capacious bag, all stock in trade for a burglar: Di's dull cotton scarf ripped into shreds to bind the bloody wrist that Tabitha raised obediently. They were a team, Steven and Di, he lifting her down all those stairs, she bringing Winifred's hat and her bags, as well as her own. Di had found the address in the handbag, repeated so many times, on so many cards and bits of paper; it must be the right address. Keys on a fob; are these the right ones? Steven asked her. Tabitha nodded. Di packed up and wiped down rapidly, removing as many traces as she could. Down, down, down, they went, past the silent waitress woman with the cup of tea in her lap and the painted smile on her face. Closed the fire door, carefully and absolutely.

The car park for council officials, smokers or otherwise, remained empty, apart from Steven's obvious car and the van hired by Sarah.

'How vulgar,' Winifred murmured, proving she was alive before letting Steven put her into the front seat where she curled like a cat.

Later, they watched her asleep. They had cleaned up the wound on the wrist, sponged her hair, Steven the natural nurse. It was a small, terraced house, only a mile from the museum in radically different territory, reminding Di of Dixon Avenue. Di raided the cupboards, found bandages and saline. She had the feeling someone had been nursed in this house; she knew the signs. Tabitha's house was immaculately organised, obsessively clean and logical, making it easy. Nothing to do then, but keep guard and consider what to do next. No question of hospital, Tabitha vetoed that. There were other scars on her wrists. Di was sitting in a clean place, on the outskirts of this town, getting towards eleven at night, looking at the most glorious selection of small paintings she had ever seen outside her own and was wondering how many of them were stolen, which ones had been taken from the museum, while thinking of Steven who sat with her, neither of them saying much. She was full of admiration for a man who had embraced a distressed, bloodstained harridan with real compassion and without thinking why. One who did not mind being covered in blood and whose first reaction was pity before judgement.

'Shame about your suit,' she said.

He shrugged, smiling. 'I've got other suits.'

'What made you react like that? What made you? Was it . . . to save *me*?'

He turned his slow smile on her.

'At first,' he said. 'Only at first, for a moment. I could see you were winning. You didn't need saving. *She*, this one, needed saving from herself.'

'The embrace,' she said, wondering at it. 'The tenderness. Where did it come from?'

'It was because of what you said. You'd just told her her brother had died. She would have been in such pain, worse than any wound. The pity of it got me. I suppose I was thinking of how I would feel if anyone told me I'd lost you. I'd be screaming and banging my head against stone. I'd need someone to stop me.'

A moment's silence while Di adjusted the rug on Tabitha's knees.

'Even though you aren't my brother?' Di said.

'Even though. No, I'm not your blood brother. But you're the centre of my world and if anything happened to you, I'm not sure I'd want to be alive. How long have you known?'

'A long time,' she said. 'DNA testing, that stuff, I did it first.'

'And you still want to know me?'

'Especially now.'

'Be still my beating heart,' Steven said, striking his chest.

The old lady in the armchair facing them, tucked in with the rug over her bandaged arm in a sling, opened her eyes and looked directly at them both.

'Did you get that painting you wanted to see?' she said to Steven.

'Yes,' he said, quietly. 'And I've brought it back. And we're going to bring back Toby's paintings, too. And when we do, that Director is going to have a major exhibition with all of them on the walls, you wait and see.'

'Promise?'

'Promise. Cross my heart and hope to die.'

'How will you make him do it?'

'Blackmail. Plenty of that, plus persuasion. Plus maybe proving what a gallery like this could do and why it's worth it.'

There was the ghost of a grin.

'That was what I wanted,' she said. 'Not everything I wanted, but enough.' She shuffled upright, suddenly animated.

'But you'd better take them now, the other ones I took from the store. That wall, over there. Take them now. The whole wall. Take them now, before I stop believing you. Take them NOW. I've been going a little mad, just a little dotty. You must take them now, so you can bring them all back together. Nothing is safe with me. Take them *now*.'

They could see that Tabitha had only brought into her house the smallest and the most portable. More signed TH, Disher, Nash, Devas, things collected with a discriminating, eclectic eye by previous directors of the Kemsdown. It felt entirely strange to take the pictures off the walls, out of the front door and transfer them underarm into the boot of Steven's car. It felt like theft, but it was necessary theft and both felt as conspicuous as if they were on stage. Beware the Dixon Avenues of quiet towns. Di found she could use her injured hand painfully.

'You can go now,' Tabitha said. 'I'll be all right. Come back tomorrow. I shan't die in the night. I'm not going to die until I see his paintings on the walls and that's a promise. I need to be alone.'

Outside, it was moonlight. Steven drove back to the council car park, where the hired four wheel-drive still stood. Twelve small paintings efficiently transferred into the capacious boot. This may be the route to bring all of them away and bring them back.

'You don't make false promises,' Di said to Steven. 'So why would the Director put the paintings on the walls when we bring them back? Why would he suddenly have a show of paintings?'

'He won't have any choice,' Steven said. 'He's in big trouble. He's overseen theft and sabotage and he's accountable, however much they cut his budget. Who is Winifred Doris?'

'The museum's mascot. The woman who sits between rooms, watching and sipping tea if you feed her a penny. The Director's nemesis. I wonder what Sarah's doing?'

'I hope,' Steven said, 'that she's still seducing the Director. I have no worries about Sarah. More about you – you're hurting, aren't you. You've got rooms booked, you said?'

'Will you stay, Steven, will you stay?'

'I'm not going now,' Steven said decisively, cradling her arm. 'We have a mission to complete tomorrow.'

The Director was indeed a man in trouble. He had needed alcohol like he needed breath. He had the chronic thirst of emotional dehydration. After half a bottle of wine in the subtly lit bar of the hotel where Sarah had booked herself and Di for the night, he gave up trying. The light in there flattered Sarah and her made-up eyes while not enhancing his pale skin. After half an hour, he gave up pretending he could sustain a conversation about how to film installation art, and Sarah had run out of questions on a subject about which she knew nothing and cared less. His gestures slowed down from effusive to small movements of the fingers and his replies became slower. He could not take his eyes away from her sympathetic gaze; brown, soulful eyes blinking behind his slightly ridiculous glasses. Sarah felt as if she was conducting an orchestra of one. She had the impression of a man who had modelled himself on someone else and was failing to live up to whatever the role model was. He was on prototype three and it wasn't working and he was not a married man any more; that much was established. Finally, he broke eye contact and looked down at the hands twitching in his lap.

'Any favourites among the paintings you hold?' Sarah asked.

He was staring at his fingers.

'No. I find them deeply irrelevant. The automated models, another matter. Applied art with a commercial purpose, far more honest, but ... '

The voice trailed away and he shuddered, as if the very mention of paintings was fearful. He raised his glass uncertainly, spilling the wine, and watching the small spill as it spread across the table, unable to do anything about it.

'I thought it was over,' he said. 'I thought it was over. I thought she was gone. But she hasn't, she's come back.'

A tear fell from the inside of his glasses to join the wine spill on the table. *Ah*, Sarah thought: *here's progress* and felt mean for thinking it. She needed the man to unravel although she did not relish the witnessing of it, but hey, needs must. She leaned forward and touched his restless hands. He folded them around hers and held on, tightly.

'I hoped it might be the cleaner. It isn't, of course. Someone is there before I am in the morning or during the night, intercepting my mail and my email. Very random, you understand; not every day or every week. Seems to pick up on what I've ignored, see what I mean?'

She did not quite see, but gazed believingly, her own black-lined eyes full of understanding.

'And then I send panic-stricken emails to people requesting to see paintings I know aren't there any more, and I can't trace. Because all the records are buggered and I never took any notice. I thought she'd stopped.'

'How awful. What does your curator have to say?'

He looked up, puzzled. She handed him her half full glass and he drank it in one gulp.

'There isn't a curator. She left. I've got timeshare receptionists who come and go as they please. Then there are the volunteers, and I had to get rid of most of them, useless and obstructive. And then I have my nemesis, my saboteur, and no one to tell.'

'Now you have,' Sarah said, softly. 'In strictest confidence.'

'I'd better go back,' he said, suddenly embarrassed. 'It's late, I'd better go back. Though God knows, it terrifies me. I don't want to go home, I don't want to go back to the museum. She's everywhere. I thought she'd stopped,' he repeated. 'But she's started again.'

Nine o'clock. Too soon for him to go back: Di might still be there.

'Is this Winifred Doris?'

He looked puzzled.

'Winifred Doris? Oh, she'll be standing guard all right. You are so kind. Nobody's been this kind to me in three years here. Perhaps except Winifred Doris. At least she allows me to pat her head. No, I know who my tormentor is, I just *don't know what to do.*'

He didn't go, nor did he release her hand.

'You can always stay here,' Sarah said, softly. 'You'd be very welcome. Start again tomorrow, hey?'

Needs must and he had soulful eyes. She did relish a man in trouble. She knew what he was. A misguided man, probably hired as much for inadequacy as forcefulness. Someone who had lost control over the institution he was supposed to manage, and perhaps done things of which he was bitterly ashamed. An egotist though, *my* tormentor, others all useless and obstructive to My plans. And whatever it took, he was going to tell her all about it. Then she was going to supply a way to save this naïve man from himself.

'Stay for dinner,' she suggested. 'Then, if you still feel you have to go back, I'll come with you. We need more wine, how awful, what a terrible time you've had.'

It was only about paintings, not about life and death. Later, when she detoured to repair her eyes for round two, softer and smokier this time, she got the text from Di and Steven. She had seen them coming in.

Di and Steven? Well, well well. Good.

Everybody safe.

See you in the morning at six, ok?

Chapter Twelve

All very quiet on the home front. Suspiciously so. Di had only been away for a day and a night and it felt like forever.

'Listen,' Jones said to Saul at breakfast, 'never mind wondering about what those women are doing, and the messages you've been sent, mightn't it be a good idea if you fucked off for a few days? Don't you worry, the pictures will be safe. You've been spending too much time in the cellar and you know walking by the sea depresses you. Go on, fuck off to London, you need a fix. Better not to be here when they get back.'

Saul seized the suggestion. Jones even took him to the train, to stop him looking over his shoulder all the time, the way he had when he had walked back down the pier as a demoralised man. It was good to have him out of the house, allowing Jones to contemplate and let his floating thoughts form themselves into conclusions. Jones needed empty space for that and he was best working on his own.

He was thinking to himself, *They're going to have this exhibition in three or four months' time, down in this bloody basement that is currently housing stolen goods. No matter the lack of intention to permanently deprive, that's what they are, stolen goods, and you can't have the public alongside stuff like that, especially not when there's someone out there who knows, and someone surely does. Not only that, Di can't have young Patrick staying when there's stuff like that in the house. Not fair on anyone, though I quite see why they took them. Di and Sarah were daft to do what Saul said and go back for the sketches, only for the dog to ruin them, that was rich that was. Who was it she smelt? Was it Toby Hanks, or was it Quig? Was that stupid fucking dog angry or sad?*

It was also occurring to Jones that the delivery of the sketch to Saul on the pier could be as much a message to himself as to Saul. It was letting Jones know what the message sender knew and issuing a challenge. Quig knew the paintings were down there because Quig was watching. Quig could easily put in an anonymous call, as if. Quig was letting Jones know that he had dangerous knowledge. By a process of elimination, it had to be Quig. There was no one else it could be.

*

Jones was standing in the glorious cellar that he admired greatly, not so much for what it had become, but because he could remember what it was. A place of shelter for the dispossessed. Dank and cold and compartmentalised and twice filled with flooding seawater; to fatal effect on one occasion, and after that, the place was a sort of grave for ten years. Best to draw a veil over all of that, as everyone had done, himself in particular. He could never quite feel the same way about Peg since she had removed the bones. Peg was the very opposite of sentimental: she did not respond to atmosphere, fierce little thing, she was very good at forgetting, but then she had much less to remember. Jones could not forget the night when Gayle and Edward came in to steal and Edward smashed the place up, any more than he could forget the night, a decade before that, when Di had been caught. He had more to remember than the others; he had known this cellar when he was a boy. So had Quig. Saul was better placed to eradicate any memory inconvenient to the furtherance of his plans. The cellar was a magnificent exhibition space and that was all he either saw or felt. It was what it was now: it had no past, only a future. And now, the stolen paintings contaminated it all over again. Jones shook his head. One way and another, this was becoming the wrong place to hold an initial exhibition, especially one that featured the word 'guilt'.

Jones could hear Peg upstairs talking to Grace as they

pottered round the kitchen, vague sounds, as if coming from a distance. She'd be going out later. He could have done with some company on his current mission, to go to Dixon Avenue and look at the burned-out house where Toby Hanks had lived and where, he was slowly coming to conclude, Quig still lurked. Jones was grateful that Sarah Fortune, whom he liked more and more, kept him fully informed and told him things she was not supposed to tell, such as Di being pushed over on the cliffs on the day Toby Hanks died. Couldn't be Quig, but Quig might have been there. And about Toby Hanks' last instructions, and about how the raid to get the sketches had really been a bit of a botched job, because she had left so many traces. And about Quig being in touch with those bastards, Patrick's parents. Sarah did not believe in keeping secrets: Sarah knew Jones's worth, his value. Di did not like telling him stuff that might worry him, while Sarah had no such inhibitions. Sarah knew you needed every ally you could get and she was not going to let him get out of this story. Jones was not sure if he was happy about that, but there really wasn't any choice. He was back in the story because Quig was.

Something else Sarah had said. 'Look,' she said, 'wouldn't it be better to get Di's father alongside? Isn't it better to have the enemy where you can see him?'

Perhaps.

What were they doing, those women? Only researching?

Not breaking and entering? Dear God, don't let them get arrested. Don't let Di go to prison again, not even for a day. He was thinking all this on the way to Dixon Avenue, a place none of them knew any more, even if they ever had. Another world, away from the sea, the other side of the tracks from whence Di came, and her father. The bad-lands of any English town. De-communitised piece of social development and he didn't understand why it was that one road thrived while another didn't. Why, on his beat, more were arrested in Dixon Avenue than anywhere else. He was thinking like a fisherman, of how some people got away with it scot free, and others sank; how some fish came to the surface and said, *catch me, eat me,* while others swam away. It looked like Quig had always got away with it; feckless, owning-nothing, respecting-nothing Quig, but had he? Jones plodded along, realising, not for the first time, that he didn't know his town any more. He did not know it half as well as Peg, and perhaps he should have asked Peg, but it looked as if Peg really did want out of the story and it was better that way. Jones was no longer one of the people. Happens, when you joined the ranks of the privileged, with a room in the big house, and your own rented flat.

And Quig? What was it like for Quig? What did Quig have when he was at home? Sweet fuck all. Never bothered to own anything, that was Quig.

Although, from what Sarah had told him, Quig had

Toby Hanks. Or Toby Hanks had trusted Quig in some way, was a friend of sorts, although Quig being a friend to anyone was a contradiction in terms. How little he knew. Jones was feeling that he should have come here much sooner than this, ashamed for leaving it so long. Admitting to himself that he was a little afraid of Dixon Avenue and all its anarchy.

Looked at objectively in the light of the early afternoon and taking away those associations, it wasn't so bad. Decent enough housing if you compared it to some, each house with an open space. Maybe it was the cars that ruined it, the busy road bisecting it and turning it into a rat run. It seemed to Jones that it was better than he remembered, certainly at the end where he began. Houses here were still so cheap, it was a place to start on the property ladder; maybe it was coming up in the world. Gloom descended as he progressed to the further end where everything was rented. He stopped before no. 117, Toby Hanks' dwelling place that looked dirty rather than ruined. Only a small fire, he'd heard; specific in purpose, perhaps, to wreck and obfuscate rather than destroy. That would be Quig's style; Quig could control a bonfire as well as he knew how to set one.

Jones had come whistling up the street the way he did when he had once patrolled, making enough row to warn anyone wise enough to run away and hide. His method then had meant only the very stupid got arrested on his watch. Now he whistled for courage until he stopped by the privet hedge and saw the door of the place standing open with banging sounds coming from inside. Jones took a deep breath and followed the noise. There was someone inside who had a right to be there. What harm could befall, mid-afternoon in bright daylight, and all the same he was wishing he'd been able to bring a dog, like that sweet Alsatian he once had that looked as if it could eat your leg off but was scared of birds. A bit like himself, more bark than bite. Twitchy was an understatement; Jones was spoiling for a fight. Or rather wanted to use his fists the way you did when you were afraid.

He saw a man with a sledgehammer, attempting to smash off the tiles of an ugly, smoke-blackened fireplace in the front room, not caring who heard. Doing it badly, so that he swung the hammer and struck the edge with the recoil going back up his arm and making him reel away with dust in his eyes. Not a strong man any longer, not getting any younger, or doing a good job of it. Quig was not good at brute force, better at sneaking up behind than coming at you front on, better with an arrow and a gun than a hammer. He may as well have been hurling cannonballs at a bush. Jones could see what he was trying to do and could not bear to see a job badly done. Jones loved controlled demolition.

'Fuck's sake,' he shouted, 'give it here. You want this fireplace out, or what?'

Quig turned in surprise, handed over the hammer

without question, and Jones took it and smashed it against the ugly tiles with great precision, bish, bash, bosh, got each large tile in the centre and five minutes on, they were shards he could pluck from the cement, revealing an older fireplace behind, perhaps worth preserving, perhaps not. It was liberating, this doing something he was good at. All that precision training in knocking down doors had made a good jobbing builder out of Jones. It was satisfying, anger absorbing stuff. Quig's skills were different.

'If you remember,' Jones said, standing there, panting a bit and resting on the sledgehammer, 'it was always good fun to get into empty houses and smash things up. When you were ten and I was twelve. Happen we're a bit too old for this. Never saw you as a house renovator, Quig. Not quite your style. Haven't seen you for a year. Thought you'd gone.'

Wielding the sledgehammer calmed him right down and showed him his own stamina. He was amazed at himself at his superior strength and Quig himself was equally surprised, looking at him as if he had landed from another planet. Maybe remembering that they were once almost kin before Quig went bad. When did Quig go bad? Look at him now, man in a damaged house, looking quite at home.

'What were you going to do next before I so rudely interrupted?' Jones asked, keeping it nice and friendly. 'Not trespassing, are we?'

Quig smirked.

'It's my house. I can do what I like. I own it, and I own next door, too. You don't know much, Jones, not any more. I'm a fucking landlord, Jonesy, get used to it. Now I'm going to be a property developer, watch me.'

Jones was shocked. Quig, owner of property; well, well. And all this time he'd been thinking Quig was living on borrowed floors or chicken sheds. Jones had an exaggerated respect for those who owned property, his own long lost to divorce.

'So this is where you hide out, then?'

'I don't hide,' Quig said. 'There's no need. It's just that nobody sees me. I'm invisible. When nobody wants to see you, they just don't see, have you noticed? Last time I saw my daughter, she didn't see me at all, passed me by on the cliffs as if I wasn't there. Then she met Edward, who pushed her, and she didn't even want to hear me shout. Nobody sees me.'

Even his voice seemed to have changed into a lower octave.

'Well, blow me down,' Jones said. 'Homeowner, landlord. You haven't done so badly, have you, Quig? I'm impressed.'

And so he was. Jones remained leaning against the sledgehammer. Quig was seated. Jones could have brought down the sledgehammer on Quig's head and Quig knew perfectly well that he wouldn't. It was Quig's house and Jones was a guest.

'So what do you want to know? You haven't come for nothing, you never do.'

It was ever the same with Quig. He always got you straight on to the back foot.

'About you sending messages,' Jones said.

'That sketch? To that little turd who comes in here before Toby's gone cold and takes all his best paintings? Yeah, I watched the little fucker. I was next door waiting for him, see?'

'Friends?'

'Sort of. No, more than that. Drinking friends. I could do with a drink. I was coming round for the rent that night. As soon as I saw that turd, I knew Toby was dead. I knew where he was, how ill he was. Poor old bugger always said he wanted to die with a brush in his hand. So I let the little turd do what he was doing, then I found his sketch and kept it. Taxi driver told me where he went with the stuff and I made the connection. And then, blow me, my own thieving daughter comes back for the rest. And cleans her dad's house for him! Couldn't believe it.'

He laughed. 'I thought, there you go, girl, back on form. Only what were they taking all that rubbish for? Didn't get it. Toby didn't rate it, was going to burn the paper. And that daft bitch with her, making all that noise, and leaving her gloves and her hat and her DNA. Amateurs. Then I thought I'd set a little fire, cover their tracks. Silly of me.'

'You set a fire? To cover *their* tracks? In your own house?'

'Yes. Not very clever. Wasn't thinking. I only wanted to help. I don't want my daughter going to prison for nicking a pile of rubbish, wouldn't be right. For a big heist, maybe, not for something like that. Crown jewels, at least. And besides, I want those pictures back. The ones the turd took. Someone's got to deliver them on.'

Jones felt in his capacious pocket for the supply of miniature bottles of whisky he carried for his hours on the pier. Expensive way of boozing, but hey. He tossed one into Quig's lap, thinking he could spare it. A homeowner, shit.

'So you aren't going to shop them to the police?'

'Wash your mouth out, Jones. I'd never do that. I just wanted him to know I'd seen him, and that sometime or other, he was going to have to talk to me. Wanted him to know he hadn't got away with it, stealing from a dead man.'

Quig definitely had the moral high ground. They both drank, Jones sipping, Quig swallowing in one, burning his throat. The effect on him was instantaneous and Jones remembered what a poor drinker he was. Or maybe that was part of the act, like looking like a down-and-out with nowhere to go when he owned a house or two.

'Then I figured it might all work out for the best,' Quig said, already slurring slightly. 'Because I've got to get them fucking pictures back where they belong. I promised Toby

I'd do that, I promised. He made me swear on my life I would, and I did swear. Poor old bastard, sick as a parrot. Had a hole in his heart, did you know.'

Jones tossed him another of the little plastic bottles. It dropped to the floor, and Quig looked at it for a while before leaning forward, picking it up and studying it, as if deciding if he should drink it now or keep it for later. He put it in his pocket.

'Big old hole,' Quig said. 'And you know me, Jones. I make a promise, I fucking keep it.'

Jones granted that one: yes, Quig kept promises and honoured hideous contracts, with the rider that pledges made to wives and daughters did not count. Quig was merely a quasi-criminal in a dirty, obviously lucrative trade and even if it was Dixon fucking Avenue, he owned more than Jones did. Two fucking houses. Quig unscrewed the top of the second little bottle.

'I've lost the fucking plot,' Jones said.

'Pay attention at the back,' Quig said. 'Keep a-fucking-lert. Toby Hanks had a sister he lived with, see? Squeezed him to death, he said. But was everything. Wanted him to light up the world and be famous and loved him to death, don't know how, until he couldn't stand it. Like me, like you, you can't have a woman owning you. He didn't want what she wanted for him, you know?'

He stood up and stretched his legs. Quig had legs like bent sticks. Property-owning Quig.

'But she sent his paintings after him, you know? And he didn't want them, he wanted them to go back. To fucking wherever they were, so at least someone might see them one day, he said. And I've got to get them there. I promised. And then the turd stole them. They're in Di's house, I know they are. And I know what she's like. She'll get them back. Saves me a problem. She can't sit on stolen stuff any more than she could sit on a spike.'

'So where is it they've got to go back to?' Jones asked, pretending he didn't know.

'Got to go to Winifred Doris. Place called Kemsdown, labels on the back. That's where the sister stole them from,' Quig said. 'And you know what, Jones? I was going to ask Di to help me with that one, because I sure as hell didn't know how I was going to do it. Not my area of expertise. I was going to go down on my bended knees to ask her for help when the time came. Only that day when I saw her on the cliffs when she didn't see me or hear me either. Made me angry. And then blow me, that turd, her mate, comes along and steals the stuff. Fuck me.'

Jones leaned the sledgehammer against the wall and surveyed his handiwork. Quite a nice fireplace under those nasty tiles. Not such a bad house, if it was cleared and opened out. A nice little project, sort he liked.

'It really was Toby who painted those paintings, was it?' Jones asked. 'Not someone else?'

'He said so. Did them when he was young.'

'You could do with a hand round here, I guess.'

'Not from you I don't,' Quig said, without conviction.

'Was Toby Hanks going to pay you for your trouble?' Jones asked.

'Strewth, no. Churchmouse-poor, though he always made it with the rent. I respected him for that. I liked him, you know. Perhaps because he seemed to like me. You know what? He drew me once, made me look handsome. It takes a lot to do that. Told me I had a great face and fine hair. You could love a man for less than that.'

Quig sighed. He was halfway over the yardarm with a long way to go and a short time in which to strike a deal before he went back to lying.

'Tell you what, Quig, how about this? Di will get those pictures back to the Kemsdown place, no worries. She knows how to do it and she'll do it. But there's got to be a bargain. You've got to tell me what's going on with you and Di's stepdaughter Gayle, and that shit of her husband. You've been talking to them, I know you have.'

Quig tossed the empty plastic bottle into the air, and caught it as it fell. Then he dropped it on the ground and kicked it away. It made a lot of noise in the silence.

'Why should I tell you anything about that?' Quig said. 'When you never believe that I'm only trying to help?'

'There's help and help, Quig. You were trying to help when you throttled the dog and left it on the doorstep, and what kind of help was that?'

Jones found he was shouting and immediately regretted it. Maybe, just for once, he should give Quig the benefit of doubt. Here was a guy who kept promises and never shopped anyone which made him, brute that he was, several rungs up from the bottom of the pile as far as Jones was concerned. And he owned a house, which in Jones's eyes put him in a different category. 'Sorry,' Jones said, 'sorry. Fuck it, I'm sorry. I'm in your house and I shouldn't shout. Where did it all go wrong? I'll really help you with this house, you know,' he added. 'If you want.'

'I want to go straight,' Quig said. 'I want Di to be proud of me. And for the record, Toby Hanks asked me to deal with the dog. Put it out of its misery, poor thing running wild and sick while he was in hospital. So I did. I told him it was out of its misery. He thought it was dead.'

Getting rid of dead animals, shooting rats. That was how Quig had started.

'Good of you,' Jones said, keeping irony out of his voice. 'Now about these guys.'

He offered the third and last of the miniature whiskies. Quig shook his head in refusal. He walked across the room, picked up the empty bottle and sat back in the chair, fiddling with it, not really drunk at all. Quig always had to be doing something,

'He painted me handsome, that Toby Hanks did,' Quig said. 'That's what a drawing can do, right? Showed me my own face and what I was. Once. I told him stuff I never told anyone and he still liked my face.'

Nothing to say to that. How little Jones knew and how suspicious he was, while looking round and dying to get cracking on this house.

'S'all about the basement,' Quig said. 'All about that. That's what they ask. They've always had my number from before and they called about the basement. Patrick – nice lad, Patrick – told his mum and dad about the basement, the cellar I call it, and all the works been going on there this last year. They wanted me to take a look, well, I've always been looking from the outside while it was being done and like I said, nobody ever sees me, because they don't want to see me, and, yes, I think I will.'

He held out his hand for the third miniature bottle that Jones put into his palm. Nothing left for the pier – never mind. Quig did not drink it; only warmed it in his hands, tossing it about. It might go back into his pocket with the second one, it might not. Jones waited, patience never his strongest suit, listening for the traffic in the road beyond. Quig was king here. Homeowner, not even a little bit pissed.

'They wanted to know what it looked like,' Quig said. 'Like was it recognisable from what it was before, from when Patrick's mother knew it, from when you and I knew it? Was it so different from when they went in to snatch stuff? You know they did, Jones, you were away with that

Peg in the police car, but I was there, watching. And, as far as they know, they were caught on camera, upstairs and downstairs, smashing stuff. What they want to know is, is the downstairs so different to what it was, that any fucking footage of them going mad in it would be unrecognisable? Like, made useless, because while it might be showing them, it's showing them in a place that doesn't exist any more. So, shows nothing. Do you get my meaning?'

Jones did. It made sense.

'And they also want to know about the other way in.'

'What other way in?'

'Mrs Edward says there's another way in, goes out under the road, comes out in one of the sheds. Said she remembered it from when *she* was a kid. So do I. I know that place better than anyone. I've camped out there. There's definitely another way in.'

Jones made an instant decision. He got up and put on his coat.

'You're a bad bastard, Quig, so you are. Best way, you come and look, you ready for this? Let's go now.'

'What? To Di's house, where we went to school?'

'The same.'

Let the enemy into the camp, then you can watch him. Let him be the go-between.

'She isn't there,' Jones said. 'Maybe Peg is. Can you cope?'

'I can if she can. I'd surely love to see that cellar.'

'And misreport it?' Jones asked.

'Maybe so,' Quig said. 'I'd do anything to keep those bastards off my daughter's back. They want to bomb the place. And they want the CCTV coverage of what they did, or they want it made worthless. Basically, if they can't have the place, they can't bear for it to succeed.'

'You don't want it bombed yourself?'

'My daughter's house? You kidding? Why do you think I got the money out from under the bed and bought this house? She's going to be famous one day. She'll have enough to do explaining her own past. I don't want her to have to explain me.'

There was the same, not-so-silent taxi driver who might have driven Saul from the scene of the crime, appearing within minutes of being summoned, everybody's friend; another native of Dixon Avenue although he garaged his car elsewhere. So short the distance, a mere mile between these two, not even parallel universes. There was nobody in the house, not even the dog, because wherever Peg had gone, she had taken her, too. And there they were, in this reconstituted place, Jones and Quig, admiring a haven where they had once hidden as schoolboys, smoking.

'This might be where it began,' Quig said. 'Old headmaster, or someone, called me in to kill the rats in this dump. I must have been fourteen. Look at this.'

Theatre. Quig was wandering round in the space,

genuinely entranced, and Jones, seeing it afresh through someone else's eyes, was impressed by the fact that both Quig and he seemed to have developed the ability to admire the curving space and the elegant stairs.

'But where's the old back door?' Quig said. 'The one that went over the road?'

'In your dreams,' Jones said, not remembering.

'Smugglers' tunnel, before there was a road in front. Blocked off. Never block off anything, I say. Sea always comes in, always did. Well, if that thieving turd got all this done, he can't be that bad, but he never knew how it was. These Toby's paintings, hey? Can't say I ever looked, don't think he did either, but they look good here. He told me his sister had two dozen more. They were too smothering close and he had to get away from her. So it goes. I can see a lot of them would look good together, don't you think?'

There was Quig, going round like a blind man, touching brickwork, his head sometimes lit by the artful spotlights in the ceiling specifically designed to bisect the room and illuminate art on walls, his rather magnificent hair offsetting his hard-man face as he tapped on the surfaces, placing his hands on warm brick as if he loved it. He looked as different at one end of the room as he did at the other.

He turned to Jones, getting all emotional. 'Look what she's done,' he said. 'Look what's she's done. Going to be great. Can't let them fuckers ruin it. But they're going to be mad as snakes when they see it. 'Cause it should all be theirs. Can't let this happen, can they? This ain't the best place for the first outing, is it? And it ain't been done quite right. Goes a bit too much for being grand and pretty, see what I mean? They haven't blocked off the water. And there isn't enough slope to the drain.'

Sounds from above. The door at the top of the steps to the kitchen was open. Jones could identify Sarah singing, her voice high and light.

Chapter Thirteen

Sarah was still singing when she came down the stairs into the cellar from the kitchen looking for her brother, looking for anyone, and glowing.

'Hello,' she said, stopping halfway down and leaning over the curved rail.

'Meet Mr Jack Quigly,' Jones said. 'Di's father, to you. Is she with you?'

'No. Is this wise, Jones?'

Sarah was the only one who had never actually met Quig before although she knew exactly who he was, and was wondering briefly what Di's reaction might be if she found this hated person in the house. Until she remembered that Di had been rethinking her father, who did not look particularly nasty or scary in this kind light.

'Quig, who was Toby Hanks' last known friend, has interesting information,' Jones said loudly. 'And he didn't sneak in, I invited him.'

Sarah nodded and her frown cleared into a smile. If Jones had issued an invitation, that was OK, and yet again, Jones was grateful to her for trusting his judgement and keeping him informed. Leaning over the elegant rail Saul had installed in lieu of the utilitarian banister, she looked like a sweet avenging angel with her hair on fire. Quig was staring at her as if she was a heaven-sent apparition. Already profoundly impressed by the room, he was now mesmerised. When Sarah threw a leg over the curved rail and slid the rest of the way down simply to save time, his enchantment was complete. She approached gracefully, holding out her hand.

'Nice to meet you at last,' she said to Quig. 'Though I've never heard anything good about you. It's all been shite.'

'Nothing good to tell,' Quig stammered, letting his hand be shaken. It was a hand that had touched more carrion than he could remember; he felt grubby in this space and yet this angel grabbed his paw and shook it heartily.

'Where's Di?' Jones asked, worried that she might be bringing up the rear and uncertain of her reaction if she did. 'She all right?'

'Never better, I'd say. Staying in this Kemsdown place. In heavy negotiation with the Director of a certain museum about the return of certain paintings. And possibly creating an exhibition.'

There was laughter in her voice. They must have had a result, Jones thought, because Sarah was triumphant.

'I better go,' Quig said. 'Got to go. You got things to talk about.'

'Toby Hanks' friend, hey?' Sarah said, beaming at him. 'Looks like he needed one.'

'Yes, I think he did. He wanted me to do something for him.'

'I know.'

Jones was amazed that Quig failed to recognise Sarah as someone he had seen before. She must be better at disguise than he realised or Quig was less observant than he thought. He was grinning and Sarah was being shockingly positive and friendly, something to which Quig was entirely unaccustomed.

'I got drawn by Toby Hanks,' Quig stammered, still gazing at her. 'He did me proud. Made me look at myself.'

'Really?' Sarah said. 'You and I both got drawn by Toby, I knew we had something in common. He was good, wasn't he?'

'Wouldn't know how to judge,' Quig said, scuffling his feet. 'But he was a good man to know. Look, I'd better be off.'

'See you out,' Jones said.

They went out through the back end of the house to

the narrow road behind, the way they had come in, and Quig was saying, 'Christ, who's she? She's a bit nifty, she is. She's lovely.'

'Welcome to the Enterprise,' Jones said. 'If this place comes to harm, it comes to her, too. Are you with us or against us? Are you in or out?'

'I always wanted to be in,' Quig said, quietly, looking down at his dirty shoes.

'You could've fooled me on that one,' said Jones. 'I'll be round with some tools, tomorrow. Don't do anything till then.'

Seven in the evening, with the sky getting lighter. Jones stood on the doorstep, watching home owning, sleep-walking Quig move away from the place where they had once been at school with a spring in his step, despite the limp. Jones was thinking, *Hey, Di's got it right, give us a touch of beauty and we come right. Give us the pride of ownership and we never look back. Beauty does it, civilises us, even beautiful brickwork. Di's right; we need art and beauty and property. We all need this place. And by the way, there is another entrance to the beautiful cellar that someone else knows about apart from Quig.*

Sarah was humming at the kitchen table while writing a list in a big, round hand. She really was such a creative tart.

'Right,' Jones said, glad to be alone with someone who thought as pragmatically as he did most of the time. 'You tell and I'll tell. You look like a woman who just been laid for the first time in ages. Speaking for myself, I've forgotten what it was like though I do remember the smile.'

'A pleasure grossly exaggerated if you confuse it with true love,' Sarah said. 'Never to be ignored, all the same. Anyway, I didn't need to get carnal with my target, that Director. He was too drunk and maudlin by the time we got to that point, but all the same I do feel a bit empowered, because he sang like a canary, poor man. He's in big trouble because he's let half the paintings the museum owns go missing. Ignored them, never showed them, even tried to sell some, and then Winifred Doris came to haunt him and stole some more. Now there's an audit coming up and he's got to get them back, something like that. So we have him where we want him. Or Steven and Di do. Steven will be putting him through it as we speak.'

'You'll never make a good thief, Sarah, my love. No precision. Can you start at the beginning and go on to the end? Like as if you were telling a story to a simple man, like me? You sound like you were talking to Saul, not me.'

'I need a drink,' Sarah said. 'Sorry. Tell me about Quig. What was he doing here? Does he no longer count as a bad man?'

'No, he's still a bad man, but he might just be a bad man capable of doing something good. He took a shine to you, though. Don't suppose you'd consider having a go at civilising him, would you?'

'By what means?' Sarah said innocently, pulling the cork out of a bottle. 'I never say never. If there was no other way to avert disaster without doing damage to the dynamic of this household, I'd certainly consider it. Otherwise not. He has very nice hair and he might brush up well.'

'He saw you and Di collecting the sketches from Toby's house. Quig owns that house and the one next door. I only just found out. But he didn't recognise you today – I wonder why?'

'Must be the makeover,' Sarah said, carelessly. 'Owns two houses, did you say? A homeowner! Well, that could be another matter altogether. That makes him eligible. Was that all he saw?'

'No. He saw your brother Saul stealing the twelve paintings on the night Toby died. Even by Quig's standards, that was pretty disgusting behaviour. He can identify him.'

Sarah put the bottle of wine down on the table with a thump.

'Ah, I see. Now we have a balance of power situation. He can identify my brother as a thief and put the whole thing in jeopardy. He could tell Patrick's parents, who could use that to blow up the ship. He could tell the police. Is that why you're being so nice to him, asking him round? It's certainly a reason for me to be very nice to him indeed. *Extremely* nice.'

Jones hesitated.

'No,' he said. 'No, it wasn't quite like that. He's changed. Buying a house changed him, it does that. He's got a lot to lose now. And somehow Toby Hanks changed him. He told me Toby Hanks thought he was handsome. Seems to me this Toby has redeemed a lot of people.'

They sat and thought about it in silence, listening to the ticking of the kitchen clock.

'Tell me the story,' Jones said. 'Di's coming back when?'

'Tomorrow, I should think. She's staying a while with Winifred Doris. Steven will go back. That's another chapter, Jones. He's turning out rather well. And he isn't her brother. Oh shit! How could I forget? Help me, Jones. I've got a boot full of paintings. How could I forget?'

She raced out of the back door and Jones followed. He saw that she had backed the car into the yard with the capacious boot almost at the door. She lifted the hatch and Jones recoiled. Framed paintings of various small sizes, neatly stacked in pairs with the canvas on the inside, not wrapped or protected in any way with visible labels on the reverse. 'Quick,' she said. 'Quick. Get them in before anyone sees. How could I forget? It's that Quig, he distracted me.'

Because Jones had had enough shocks for the day he was biddable. Instead of protesting he did as asked, carried the paintings inside and into the cellar, leaning them against the brick walls alongside the others, furious with himself for doing it and shielding his eyes. They made short work of it and returned to the kitchen where Sarah finally poured from the bottle.

'What the hell do you think you're doing?' Jones grumbled, grasping a tumbler. 'You went off to investigate how to return stolen goods, and what do you do? You bring in a whole lot more.'

'There wasn't any choice, you see,' Sarah said reasonably. 'Winifred Doris insisted they took them out of the house immediately, last night I mean. There was nowhere else to put them. Nothing else to do but for me to bring them back here while they deal with the Director. We decided that this morning at the dawn debrief. It's a very temporary arrangement, and then they'll all be returned together.'

Jones groaned, unable any longer to read between such hectic lines.

'Here we are,' he said heavily, 'even more like hostages than ever. We got double the number of stolen paintings.'

'No intention to permanently deprive,' Sarah said. 'Not quite the same thing. We are merely acting as agents.'

'Tell me how it all happened, from the beginning to the end.'

'Yes,' Sarah said. 'Yes I shall. But I've just thought of something else to do with Mr Quigly. Supposing, when the time comes, and it has to be soon, we get Quig to return all the paintings to the Kemsdown? Drive them there, be the delivery man. That's what he was supposed to do, what Toby Hanks asked him to do. And that way, he'd be thoroughly compromised, wouldn't he? Complicit in not-quite-legal activity. He couldn't tell anyone then, could he? Would he do it, do you think?'

'Yes,' Jones said. 'Yes, I think he would.'

Women, Jones thought, *are fiendish*. What a pity it was impossible to live without them.

There he was, the Director, sitting in his office, hungover, deserted by his friend of the night who disappeared before breakfast, leaving him with instructions to be in his office at midday. Which he obeyed because he could not do otherwise. He sat there, feeling queasy and lonely and more than a little confused, facing two people, a man and a woman. Both good-looking, one of them a little bit famil-iar, the other with a voice of command. They were demanding a full and frank exchange for which he was not ready. Devoid of authority, he wanted to be anywhere else. He wanted to be either dead or still in the bed he had left.

'This is the narrative,' said the man, 'that's been pieced together from several sources. In the beginning, when you were appointed, you had precious holdings of local and national artists that you wanted to ignore for the sake of a new innovative gallery. So you did ignore them and left a volunteer to manage the store. You attempted to sell some of them, which you had no right to do, and then you denied their existence. You took no notice of the opinions of the staff. You wanted to do your own thing and not be burdened by old stock. You didn't listen, you alienated. Fair dos, the bosses kept cutting the budget, but it was you who cut it on staff and security. Please contradict me if I'm wrong.'

His tone was persuasive, non-judgemental, understanding, as if he wanted to be a friend. His stained and crumpled clothes did not detract from his authority.

The Director did not contradict; instead sat looking and feeling like a rabbit in headlamps. All the same he felt relieved; he wanted to give up the fight and let someone else make the decisions.

'Then one of the volunteers you'd alienated came to haunt. She found out you'd been attempting to sell paintings as well as failing to look after them and not showing them and that made her mad.'

'I'm afraid I don't remember the volunteers. As volunteers, they did as they do, they went. They were obstructive.'

'You have a talent for ignoring the small fry or perhaps just not knowing,' the man said kindly. 'You dispensed with her services. Anyway, she is the obsessive sister of one of your finest artists, Toby Hanks. You had a dozen of his in the store. Little known, but a rather brilliant, could I say, *innovative* artist in his way. Anyway, his sister was deeply hurt that her brother's paintings were never shown and that you didn't even acknowledge their existence. This woman regarded paintings as living things, kept in prison and starved of oxygen. So she removed them and sent them to her brother, because then, at least, someone would see them. She had other motives too. She was seeking rapprochement, some sort of forgiveness, perhaps.'

The Director fumbled for the cigarette he could not have.

'She infiltrated the whole system,' the man continued. 'She became equally indignant about other, ignored artists you have. Looked at your emails at three in the morning, probably. You never quite mastered the logging off, did you? And you were too proud to ask for help. You've always been careless with enquiries, because you thought the paintings were in the way: you weren't interested in them, why should anyone else be? Double insult for the lover of paintings. Not only were you hiding them, but you weren't allowing anyone even to research them.'

He paused.

'Your one-time volunteer removed other paintings, too, small ones she liked. Recently, she was just beginning on a mad course of action to send the actual paintings to the people who enquired about them, me included. She was losing the plot, just a bit, becoming violent in her approach. She considered she was freeing things. A bit like an animal rights activist, only with art.'

'I'd like to kill her,' the Director said.

'Believe me, the feeling is entirely mutual and she is perfectly capable of killing you. In the meantime,' the man went on, 'online enquiries made it easier for anyone to ask about paintings and finally extended to you. I enquired, Mrs Porteous here enquired. Enquiries you ignored were intercepted.'

Mrs Porteous? Slowly, she swam into focus. That ghastly assistant to kind Mrs Wisegarten, whose note had said, *It will all be all right, if only you keep this appointment this afternoon. Be in your office at midday.*

'Mrs Porteous here is a major collector of British painting. She made enquiries of you and encountered Toby Hanks' sister. Mrs Wisegarten is Mrs Porteous's assistant. You are very lucky they arrived when they did.'

The Director put his head in his hands and groaned.

'To remind you,' the man said, 'I'm Steven Cockerel. I have quite a bit of money and several contacts. I'm also a collector. Ms Hanks sent me this.'

He flourished a mangled canvas. The Director shrank from it, as if he was being handed a bloodied glove.

'The trustees,' Cloake muttered. 'I have to answer to the trustees. The trustees have always supported me.'

'That support, if it still exists, and research tells me it's been waning away, will turn on its head when they realise that you've jeopardised the whole permanent collection. Who will they blame for damage like this? You and only you. When they know what's happened, they'll sack you and sue you for the loss. You'd be lucky to escape imprisonment. Disgrace, no prospect of getting another job.'

Silence fell. The Director watched them watching him and wanted to weep. He had done his weeping with lovely Mrs Wisegarten who had left so early in the morning. *I'll help you*, she said, and he had believed her. *You must trust them; they are very innovative people.*

'Who'll tell the trustees?'

'I shall, we will, of course. Unless you accept our help.'

'There's an audit in four months' time,' Cloake mumbled. 'An inspection. I don't know what to do.'

'Plenty of time,' Steven Cockerel said, smoothly, 'to put on something special. Because by that time, all the paintings, those stolen and those in the store, will be back on the walls in an exhibition featuring a retrospective of one Toby Hanks. By this means, you will be able to show what an able Curator and Director you are. Resurrecting a fine, unknown, once-local artist. Showing what you've got.'

'We might be able to help,' Mrs Porteous said. 'We could incorporate it into an even bigger exhibition. You really should look at the paintings more, you know. It really improves one's facial recognition skills. Looking at portraits, for instance, helps you to remember people.'

This was the unrecognisable Mrs Porteous in bright clothes, with bright eyes, regarding him sympathetically. Cloake touched the surface of his desk feeling for a clue, trying and failing to summon the assistance of anger.

'Where did they go?' he said.

'You don't need to know, better you don't. Someone will bring them back. And you had better advise us when to do that. Better at night, don't you think, since no one else is supposed to know they're missing? Shall we go and look at the store?'

He was in their hands and there were no choices, hating these people with fierce intensity that ebbed a little as soon as they let him lead the way as if he was still in charge. Through the empty red gallery, up the stairs, down the corridor, with Cloake thinking, *Oh God, oh God, there must be another way, I never want to go into this place again, I am ruined.*

'Such great rooms,' Mrs Porteous was saying, twitching the muslin at the windows. They passed the little waitress made of metal, sitting with her cup of tea, and he patted her capped head that always felt warm to the touch. This time, it was if she leered at him and he had always regarded little Winifred Doris as a passive, biddable friend. What was it Mrs Porteous had said? If you look at paintings, you get better at memorising faces? Not his forte; he was a man without power, stumbling into a mess of a room.

'I didn't do this,' he said. 'I really didn't do this. No, I didn't do all of this. She kept moving things about, even before I sacked her and chased her out. Then she went away, then she came back.'

Mrs Porteous touched a tiny painting of a blue horse

lying on the table. 'You may have started the rot, but the lady in question was more than uneconomical with the truth,' she said. 'She assumed another identity and came to believe it. Maybe you do the same. Perhaps we all do.'

He looked at her with renewed interest. There was not a trace of a whine in that low, conciliatory voice and the absence of it comforted him, so that he began to see a faint glimmer of hope.

'What do you want me to do?' the Director said.

'A major exhibition of paintings in three months' time,' Steven Cockerel said. 'Featuring the holdings of this museum, perhaps some loaned objects. Find an entertaining theme for it and it's going to wow them. You're going to bring in the light and the people will love you.'

'It's going to be fun,' Mrs Porteous said. 'And please do believe me, we are not your enemy.'

'I'll need a lot of help,' he said hesitantly.

'You'd have it,' she said. 'I'd love to help bring this place alive. So would Mrs Wisegarten. Can I come back later this afternoon and discuss her ideas?'

'Please,' he said. 'Please.'

It hurt to say *please*.

Steven and Di stood in the car park by Steven's conspicuous car.

'I've got to go back,' Steven said. 'To be in time for Patrick. Worried wee man, he is. I told you he phoned yesterday. Something about his father and the basement. We're supposed to be going to the Foundling this evening.'

'Then you must,' she said.

'Don't want to leave you.'

'I promised to go back to Tabitha. And I'm going back to the Director first.'

'I think I know what you have in mind, but I'm not going to ask. You like this place, don't you? You really like it and you want to save it. Was I a bully?'

'You were persuasive and masterful,' she said, meekly.

'I love you more than I can ever say. And wasn't that little blue horse beautiful? I saw you hovering. I wondered if you would take it, because I almost did. I love you, Mrs Porteous. You are my past and my future.'

Di watched him go. She felt dull in his absence, missed him immediately, and the pain in her sprained wrist was suddenly intense.

There it was. She had not entirely lost her instinctive desire to steal. She so wanted to put that little painting of the blue horse into her bag and could easily have done so. It would probably never have been noticed in the greater scheme of things. She had not even taken the chance to keep it for a little while, and then bring it back, but Lord, she had wanted to take it home.

Di was mourning the loss of an acquisitive nerve and it was like losing the sensation in a fingertip. She had lost her ruthless urge to acquire and was diminished by it. Then she thought of Steven and what he had observed of her, and dwelt on not what she had lost, but what she might have gained. She did not want to acquire: she wanted to consolidate and build on what there was. She wanted *their* exhibition to be here.

Steven – compassionate, forceful Steven. They had the same eye for the same thing. He was lovely to lie alongside, if only to sleep. He was a controlling man; something she would have to watch because, love or not, she was not going to be controlled. Her own instincts were the best and she was following them now, alone.

Di Quigly, aka Mrs Diana Porteous, went back inside to reassure the Director that she could well be the best thing that could happen to his failing gallery. She had certainly come to like this place and she did not want it to fail. It was more important than any individual ego or plan. So, she gave the Director the idea of the theme for the exhibition *he* was going to have in his lovely, light-filled spaces. She told him how the idea had been devised by a twelve-year-old who wanted to draw in people of all ages. She gave it away, and hoped the others would see her point of view, especially Patrick. All this was done following instinct; her own instinct. She had often found in the past that her own instincts had a solid foundation that was only apparent later.

It would simply be better to have the exhibition here

because it would achieve more. It would put the Porteous pictures on show to more people and it would redeem the place. She was also doing what she imagined her own darling Thomas would have done.

Then she went on to see Tabitha Hanks.

Tabitha Hanks? Winifred Doris? Are you in?

CHAPTER FOURTEEN

Patrick was sorry he had phoned Steven yesterday. He'd gabbled, shouldn't have phoned at all. It made him seem needy.

He did not mind the fact that Steven had not been there at his funny flat above the old bank when he had called him on his phone yesterday. It was just that he couldn't get Di. No, that wasn't it. He had wanted Steven because Steven was cool and knew what Patrick's dad was like. Didn't matter that he wasn't there; silly to expect it, because people worked, didn't they? Like him going to school. No adult was available every time you wanted them any more than he was himself. And they already had this plan for today.

Today, he wanted to talk about fathers and mothers

and stuff that had been brooding. Steven was the only person who might get it because Steven knew them and Steven was a man.

Patrick was early and Steven was late. Patrick hung around reading the literature about the place, interested and appalled, immediately drawn in. There was a caff and he was hungry. He looked at the display of letters and mementos and pictures and found the orphans more than a little romantic. At least none of them had a mother like his, as bitter as the lemon juice she consumed. He thought of her as a lemon and depicted his father as an angry balloon. Sometimes it was best to reduce the ones you loved to shapes so you could change them with the stroke of a pen. Steven would know about mums and dads. Steven knew everything.

Looking around at the display of photographs on the ground floor of the Foundling Museum, Patrick envied the foundlings in their clean uniforms. They looked ready to march on the world. If his mother had left him here when he was a baby he might have had a better chance, or at least, greater certainties. He would know where he was in a place like this with music in the air and pictures on the walls.

'I wish I was an orphan,' he said when Steven found him. 'Then someone could adopt me.'

'No, you don't,' Steven said, smiling. 'And I doubt if the orphans who lived here had pictures on the walls. You wouldn't want to be an orphan,' Steven repeated as they ate cheese on toast at five in the afternoon followed by cake with pistachio nuts inside, kind of green, Patrick would remember, later. 'You wouldn't want it because you need your background. Something to rebel against instead of nothing at all. The children who came here had nothing to reject and that stunts your growth. They had no one to blame, no one to accuse. Am I making sense?'

'No, not really.'

'OK. It's one thing to wish you had different parents to the ones you've got, everyone does that from time to time, but imagine what it would be like to have none.'

'It might be fun,' Patrick said, back on a food high that took away his inhibitions and made him burst out with a flood of information.

'My dad is a podge, who thinks I'm a wimp. I don't think he likes me. Sends me anywhere, to anyone, including Di, who he detests, just to get rid of me. Or that's what I thought. Now I know he lets me go so that I can spy on her. He sometimes comes and spies, too. Ever since he heard about the basement being done up, he's been pumping me for information. Nagged me, only I wouldn't, kept pretending it wasn't finished, until last time, when I knew I had to. So I took some photos on my phone, last thing on the morning we left. Felt like shit. Didn't tell Di. Since then, he's been odd. And Mum said, look what she's done to MY house. What for? And then I had to tell them about the exhibition plan. And then, Dad says, she can't do that, we won't let her do that, and Mum says, over my dead body. Dad said he'd rather burn the place down.'

He was mightily relieved to have said all that. Steven took a mental step backwards.

'You've got a dad who's disappointed in a lot of things, himself included, but at least you have a father who got you got this far and fighting. Gave you background.'

'Like the background in a painting?' Patrick asked, distracted by the idea.

'In a way. A portrait won't shine without background: it has to emerge from a background. And the whole picture will work better if it has a frame. That's what your parents give you, background and a frame. One you can leap out of and run away from. They give you the door by which to leave and the means to change and grow. Sometimes they do it by being negative.'

'While these guys,' Patrick said, waving his hand, 'had no choices?'

'Dead right they didn't. Without background, they had to go where they were sent.'

'So am I entitled to run away?' Patrick said, truculently. 'Tell me about your mum and dad. I want to make comparisons. I just wish mine might be just a bit proud of me. Tell me about yours.'

Again, that curious freeing of the mind that comes from talking while looking at something else. They had moved to the top of the building and stood gazing at a portrait of the crumpled face of Captain Thomas Coram, with his big nose, generous mouth and eyes full of amusement. He looked like a man you would want to know; kind and sharp at the same time.

'Tell me about your father,' Patrick said. 'If I tell you things, you have to tell me things back. It's only fair.'

Steven knew there was a point to this, just as there was a specific point to the phone call of yesterday. They would reach it by travelling in circles.

'Ahh. I've wasted so much time on self-pity,' Steven said, 'because the mother who brought me up wasn't my real mother. Anyway, yes, my dad abandoned me, but not until I was a lot older than you. He was an arrogant bully and I thought I hated him, but I'm grateful to him now. He made me strong. See, if you're a foundling boy, you're punching air.'

Patrick was paying close attention, focusing on details he was selecting from the information given.

'Wait a minute,' he said. 'What if Di and you got married? She's very pretty.'

'Right. Perhaps I could ask her if we ever get to know each other better.'

'And then you could adopt me.'

'It would be a great pleasure,' Steven said, gravely. 'Even without the marriage, although I think there might be a few objections. They do love you, your mother and

243

father. It's just that they don't know you very well. You puzzle them. They've yet to see what you are. Perhaps we can do something about that.'

They moved on.

'I'm glad you suggested here,' Patrick said, thinking he had maybe gone too far and wanting to redirect the subject back. 'I like it very much. It reminds me of Di's house. Bigger and older, of course, but same sort of feel.'

Grandpa's house. Home. His face clouded over.

'I think it might be because they both feel like schools. I thought it would be good to meet here because of the history of it and the scale and the way they display the pictures here,' Steven said neutrally as they moved downstairs to the ground floor parlour with its highly coloured paintings. 'Same sort of space. Shall we look, and then you can tell me what's really worrying you about your exhibition at your granddad's house? You mentioned it yesterday.'

Again a pause to consider a picture entitled *The Christening*, featuring a child dressed in lace being presented to a priest. The charm of the picture lay in the fact that it was a painting of the room in which it now hung.

'OK, I'll tell you now. It's because my father's getting madder. And my mum's losing control of him. He obsesses about Saul's basement plans. And if we do have my exhibition there, I think he'll find it unbearable, and he really will do something to stop it. And Di's dad might help, because why else are they talking? It makes me think that it would be dangerous to have an exhibition at all. And that perhaps we shouldn't do it.'

'Ah. Wouldn't that break your heart? It's based on your ideas.'

Patrick shook his head. 'Yes, it would. But not as much as worrying about my father doing something so bad that it would make it impossible for me ever to go back. And him go to prison. That really would break my heart.'

Oh, the danger of secrets. It was on the tip of Steven's tongue to repeat what he had been told about how Patrick's parents had once got into the schoolhouse, with an invitation to remove selected items. That they had wrought havoc instead, mad with jealousy. Steven knew this volatile couple teetered on the edge of self-control at all times, fantasists with a vicious sense of entitlement, these so-called friends whom he had cultivated with such calculation. He had done it at first to cheat them; it was only now that his purposes were altruistic. *I am not a nice man*, Steven said to himself. Would Di be intimidated if she knew of their current state of mind? Steven thought she should be. Would Di be angry with Patrick for taking the photographs? No, she wouldn't. Above all, they needed to respect Patrick's estimation of the risk his parents might pose to an exhibition in the basement. Perhaps Di already knew.

'Let's give that some thought, my man, while we go for a drink. I don't think you should cancel the exhibition. I don't think Di should. It's the right thing to have it, two years after your grandfather's death, and it's a great idea, but maybe it's too soon. I think it should take place, say in the autumn, but perhaps it should happen somewhere else. Not in the house. What about having it somewhere else?'

Patrick clenched his fists and thumped his chest. His glasses were crooked and he was beamingly reassured because Steven had taken him seriously and had understood. It was already dark in the street outside at seven but he behaved as if the sun had just come out.

'Is that possible? I like the basement, but I do like seeing paintings in a room with windows. They like daylight.'

'And candlelight reflecting off windows, like they do here? I know of a man who has rooms like that at his disposal and needs an exhibition just like yours.'

It was the end of a very long day. Steven wanted to speak to Di so badly, it hurt.

He also wanted to murder his so-called friends Edward and Gayle for their wilful neglect of their son.

'And there's another thing,' Patrick said in a smaller voice. 'If the exhibition was somewhere else, maybe I could ask my mum and dad to come along? They might if it was somewhere else. I'd like them to see, you know. I'd like them to see something that was my idea. Then they might look at me.'

'What a splendid scheme,' Steven said, more heartily than he felt. 'Now, where shall we go next?'

'Thank you, my dear. I've been very tired today,' Tabitha Hanks said from the depths of her chair. She had moved it so that she faced the wall of the room from which all twelve of the small paintings had been removed the night before at her insistence. To her, it seemed to have been a short twenty-four hours; to Di, the day had been interminably long and she was bewildered by how much had been achieved. She wanted to pinch herself.

'I suppose,' Tabitha said, 'that they are all really safe, along with my brother's paintings, by now. Do you promise they are?'

'Yes,' Di said, retreating to her own chair and resisting the tendency to call her Winifred Doris. 'All safely gathered in a safe place a hundred miles from here. I've checked.'

Di had done a lot of checking. Her phone was warm from the giving and receiving of information. She had spoken to everyone and they to her. There had been too much to report to rely on anything other than the spoken word.

'Cross my heart and hope to die,' she added for emphasis.

'Don't hope to die, dear. It comes round soon enough, as you know. Just don't be the last to go, it drives one mad.

Thank God for paintings living on. Tell me again how Toby died. Was there really a paintbrush in his hand?'

It was peaceful in this sterile room. The wall Di faced was pockmarked with untidy holes where the small paintings had hung and been readjusted.

'So restful, isn't it?' Tabitha said. 'Looking at an empty wall. I never knew how restful it was.'

'It looks like someone's been in with a machine gun,' Di said. 'The shoot-out at the painting corral. The Director would call it an installation.'

Tabitha began to giggle and then to laugh.

'Ach,' she said, wiping her eyes and sipping her sherry. 'Poor man, to have lived without paintings all this time. And now he's going to have to learn to love them. Tell me again how you *neutralised* him.'

'Steven "neutralised" him by blackmail,' Di said, not quite relying on Tabitha's understanding. 'And then I went back in. He was weeping. I gave him an idea, I think. Of how to have an interactive exhibition that would make people look, and both make him popular and show that you don't have to take art *too* seriously. By giving it a theme. So, it's going to be a bigger exhibition than first envisaged. Your brother's paintings are going to work better in a broader context than they would on their own. This way, they'll shine. I offered Mr Cloake a designer and a curator and the loan of fifty artworks for free. It's no good telling someone what to do if you really want them to do it. You have to take it out of their hands and say you'll do it for them. He doesn't even know how to hang paintings.'

Tabitha's gimlet eyes stared at her, curious without being unnerving. She sipped the sherry, wincing with the pleasure of it.

'I agree my brother's paintings wouldn't work on their own. They would be better noticed hanging between others. And I agree an exhibition has to have a theme. Is there a title?'

'It's "A Question of Guilt". You look at each painting and decide how innocent or guilty each depiction is. A way of looking for what it might hide or want to reveal. The idea was devised by a twelve-year-old artist.'

'I like it,' Tabitha said. 'I can see it in one of the gallery rooms. They're fine rooms, designed for paintings. Like a big house. My paintings always belonged in a house rather than a grand institution.'

Her hand wavered and the sherry spilled a little before she righted it.

'*Your* paintings?'

Tabitha was back in control and fully alert, grasping the glass with both hands.

'Only in a manner of speaking, dear, since Toby would never have painted anything without me looking after him and being his model and housekeeper. And more, of course. He thought he could exist without me, and lo, he did. Tell me, dear, did he have any friends? He was never good at making friends. Or perhaps it was me who stopped him.'

'I didn't know him, but he had a friend, and a dog.'

Tabitha shuddered. 'I'd never have let him have a dog, oh dear me, no, not when he lived with me and we had all those holes in the heart between us. Who was the friend? Don't tell me it was another woman?'

'No,' Di said. 'It was a sad, not quite bad, not quite old man. I think it might be him who'll be bringing all the pictures back.'

'I should like to meet him,' Tabitha said, her eyelids dropping. 'What's he like?'

'He has nice hair,' Di said.

She could go now but all the same she would stay until morning.

Di sat still, relatively relaxed, thinking of the weird coincidence of ideas the day had brought, as if she, Patrick and Steven had read each other's minds out of sequence, with chapters of inspiration supplied by Jones and Sarah and her own parent who had been on her mind. How, perhaps, this was all how it was meant to be.

She thought more of her father and the plentiful hair that was his one redeeming feature. How it was turning out that she was surely better off having a father than not having one at all. He had been a friend in need to Toby Hanks, Jones said. She was thinking of fathers and brothers and reflecting that this all made some sort of sense. She was trying to make sense of her own instincts.

Thought last of Toby Hanks. It was as if Toby and his paintings had influenced them all.

Exhibition in three months. Di knew you should never wish time away, but she did.

CHAPTER FIFTEEN

Picture. *A bare room with a half-closed door. Anon.*

It was three months later, towards the end of a good summer that had all been leading to this. There were seventy-four paintings to be hung in the Kemsdown Gallery over two days.

Saul did not really like the Director, Mr Cloake, and the Director did not really like him, although in a way, they liked the way the other looked. In Saul's case the Director's dress made him feel superior. Saul had an established style while the director had faux style indicating a wardrobe recently purchased off the peg. Saul's style was *ancient*, beyond vintage and acquired over time. He specialised in waistcoats and buttons, paying homage to Paul Smith as well as a succession of Edwardians, and he was perfectly comfortable in his costumes. In an email to his sister, Saul put it that this man Cloake was sartorially *persuadable* at least, sporting clothes he thought would fit an image, not quite grown-up enough to invent his own style and never entirely comfortable in what he wore. It would be the same with his taste in art. Otherwise not a bad-looking bloke for anyone in the market of a similar age and Saul wasn't, although he could see that this specimen was exactly his sister's type of uncertain male, i.e. someone who needed deconstruction and reconstruction as a man of decision. He was a person who bore the impression of the last idea that had stuck to him and by God, he needed praise.

So disappointing to find he was not as intimidating as Winifred Doris had led them to expect, although Saul knew better than to trust him. He was not harmless, merely neutralised. She, on the other hand, was a merciless creature whose existence and behaviour Saul found perfectly thrilling.

'All right,' Saul said, giving a fine impersonation of knowing what he was doing although he had never mounted an exhibition in a public place before and was relishing the challenge. He knew he was superb at hanging paintings, though. 'Quite simple. This goes there, and this goes that way. I've got the benefit of a *plan,* or should I call it a *map*? We'll lay them all out on the floor first. The benefit of this theme is that they don't have to go chronologically or in any set order. So we can hang them simply by colour and size and intuition. Such delightful rooms, aren't they?'

Saul had made himself conclude that all this was for the best, and was congratulating himself for his part in it. See? Look what *he* had done. He had been so right to spot the talent of Toby Hanks and rescue the stuff when he had. Look at the course of events he had started; everything that had happened since was because of *him*. Yet again, both he and his talent were proving as indispensable as his small, perfect self. He was vindicated. The wondrous works of TH were going to go on show with their authorship beyond doubt and that was all that mattered. T. Hanks had died and been buried and now lived again. Ownership was in the eye of the beholder and he was embarking on a new career.

It was a fine, not-too-grand space for the purpose, with window blinds diffusing the morning daylight. It was a different kind of light to that experienced by the sea, Saul thought. The eclectic Porteous pictures as well as the Toby Hanks paintings did not miss the presence of water any more than Saul did. All of them seemed happy to be here.

'Personally,' Saul said, deliberately cultivating a confiding manner and asking the Director's opinion every two minutes, 'I wasn't too sure of the *concept*, originally. So *populist*, but it will surely bring the people in. An absolutely brilliant idea of yours, so ahead of the wave. Just at the time that people are beginning to re-evaluate figurative art. Just at the time that students are beginning to protest that they aren't being taught *skills* in art school. Just at the time when some of the post-modern moguls are dying off, and all but tourists stop going to Tate Modern because it's so *boring*. The next decade is going to be more discerning about skill, don't you think? And there's this collection right on the curve. How to have fun with what you've got. I just love the *frivolity* of this. Art as a guessing game; art for people who might otherwise be watching television looking for characters in a crime novel and evidence of guilt.'

Saul loved the new role. Perhaps this was the future.

'The descriptions,' he said. 'The captions are quite brilliant. How about this one? The one that goes with this sweet old lady knitting by a fire. "Eat your heart out, Miss Marple: this woman's as sharp as needles." They make you look. Don't know how you did it.'

The Director did not laugh although he smiled without conceding that he had nothing to do with the descriptions devised by Patrick, Di and the lovely Mrs Wisegarten who had visited Kemsdown semi-frequently, each time looking subtly different and playing a different role, so that he never knew quite what to expect.

'The real value of this,' Saul said, 'is that it's absolutely *unique*. No one else has ever had an exhibition of paintings quite like this before. Globally unique.'

'Unique,' the Director murmured. 'Yes. Quite Unique.'

He had found another key word.

'I'll send the chaps away, shall I?' Saul turned on his heel, splayed his agile arms like a dancer, and said, 'OK guys, you can go now, get breakfast.' It was seven in the morning, with rainy grey light filling all the corners. The two delivery men moved off stage right, picking up the packing material as they went, sidestepping the metal waitress figure who stood guard at the door. Delivery of the paintings had been under cover of darkness, adding drama to the occasion exactly as Saul intended. One of the men yawned and the Director failed to notice when Saul winked at him. Jones and Quig, dressed in identical dungarees, swaggered out like a couple of cowboys exiting a bar.

'Right,' said Saul. 'At least they've unwrapped. So let's see what we've got. Two dozen Toby Hanks and then the Porteous collection. Plus the others from the vaults, I gather. Does that sound about right?'

'About right.'

'So seventy-four paintings to hang in the next two days! You are *brave*, Mr Cloake, you really are. Don't worry, help is at hand. We have the tools, the muscle and the eyes. Coffee, any chance? Have a look at these first, though.'

The paintings of T. Hanks laid out on the wooden floor shone like dull gold, moving in sequence from the woman with her back turned to a painting of an empty space. Cloake squinted at them.

'I'd say weirdly marvellous,' Saul went on, lecturing at great speed. 'Bordering between English Impressionist and continental Impressionistic, bridging the gap between Figurative and Abstract, with a touch of the ethereal. Also, a fantastic use of paint. Do you see how he leaves the clear ground, doesn't always fill the canvas? How he appears to be present? I'd say his major influence was Vilhelm Hammershøi, a Dane, although I'm not entirely sure, what do you think? And there's the small scale that makes all the difference: he knew his scale, this artist. Mixed with stuff on a larger scale, they'll be more noticeable, more enigmatic. Paint used to create a scene as well as an illusion. Domestic harmony and mystery, showing how much you can reveal about a faceless individual by revealing their environment. Oil paint is just so *physical*.'

What a load of bollocks, Saul thought. *But this man needs bollocks. They're just very good paintings, but he's got to buy into it. He'll remember everything I've said and repeat it to an audience with great authority when the time comes.*

'As for the rest,' he went on, 'and granted that the general theme of the exhibition – viz, a Question of Guilt, guess who's guilty – is a little lightweight, isn't it, between you and I, we go with the flow. Very clever of you to realise that we do need to have fun with art. It's the only way to beat the competition for an audience.'

'So *physical*,' the Director repeated. 'Audience competition, yes.'

'And when we've discussed the layout a little more,' Saul said, 'the chaps can come back. They're awfully handy. Oh, and by the way, do you think we could get rid of the dolls and the automata for a little while? They do get in the way.'

'Dear Winifred Doris,' the Director said, patting the head of the metal waitress in the doorway absentmindedly. 'Oh yes, they can all go back in the store.'

He was rehearsing the press release Mrs Wisegarten had written.

Play detective in this eclectic exhibition of paintings, featuring our own collection alongside loaned works. You will find revelatory portraits and scenes. In the pictures, you will find a charlatan, a cad or two, a thief, a murderess, detectives, onlookers, victims, suspects, witnesses, perpetrators, at least one murderer. It is up to you to decide how guilty or innocent each one may be and how much you like them or not.

Cloake had entirely abdicated control of the whole thing once he realised he was going to be praised. Mrs Wisegarten had been right. It was designed to make people look and disagree. The trustees loved it. Hope sprang eternal and burned bright. A question of guilt, eh? This guilt was turning into gold. And, it was free.

'What a prat,' Jones said, standing outside in the car park smoking a cigarette. 'It's the way he never looks at anyone, you know? Like you aren't anyone.'

'Don't knock it, Jones. That's a good thing, that is. A person who doesn't look you in the eyes doesn't remember you either, often a good thing. Besides, he's got terrible eyesight, didn't you notice?'

'Doesn't even say thank you for bringing them back,' Jones complained. 'Doesn't even ask where they've been these last months. Although he thinks he knows. Storage facility, quite legit, got a receipt. Face it, they couldn't stay at Di's and they couldn't come back here, because the security's shit here. I reckon they've been trying to run the place down.'

'So all the stolen stuff has been staying at my house with me on guard, right?' Quig said. 'You really sewed me up tight this summer, didn't you, Jones? Got me well in the frame as a handler.'

'You're only sewn up as tight as you wanted. You said you wanted in, and you are in, up to your neck.'

'This last three months, hasn't it gone quick?'

'That's what everyone says when they're getting old.'

'I am only thirty years old,' Di Porteous said to Sarah Fortune as they stood on the beach throwing stones. Sarah knew how the trick was to get each stone to fall into the water at the same spot. She couldn't do it. Di rarely failed.

'Is he the one?' Sarah asked, referring to Steven, throwing a stone because it was always easier to talk while doing or watching something else.

'I think so, but not yet,' Di said, casting another stone.

'Why not yet?'

'Too many reasons to count. I don't want to be owned, not by anyone or anything. I'm on a learning curve. Moving pictures out of the house makes a difference, not sure why, but it's the beginning of change. Got to let go of a lot more things before I can make a commitment to anyone. Especially to Steven. Steven wants the whole nine yards, children and everything.'

'Is it love you feel for him?'

A silly, clichéd question, Sarah thought even as she said it. Another stone entered the water. What was love, apart from a kind of neurosis, and did it have to involve ownership? Not as far as she was concerned although she had once thought otherwise. No one owns anyone any more than they owned a painting or a pet. Grace the dog roamed a hundred yards away and as soon as she realised she was alone in her landscape, lolloped back.

'Yes, of a kind. Intense feeling, liking, longing respect. Enough lust.' She laughed like an embarrassed child and picked up another stone to hold in her palm rather than throw. 'But sometimes I long for ... what I knew? The deep sleep of the married bed? Steven knows nothing about that and I do. He knows all about independence and not having to answer to anyone and I don't, not yet. Love? A profound connection, a weird way of being able to read each other's thoughts. But we aren't equals. He trusts himself. I have to learn a little more about that.'

Such a dry, objective approach to a love affair, Sarah thought, and while her pragmatic self rather approved of that, this lack of abandonment to simply being in love, shouting it from the rooftops and being giddy with it, saddened her. Here was Di loving Steven and unable to remove the ice chip embedded deep in her heart. Perhaps she could not be otherwise. All very well that she came back from her surreptitious trips to London blushing full of the joys of spring, her relationship with Steven was being conducted like a cautious, clandestine affair.

'Would you feel differently if it was all out in the open?'

Another silly question. Sarah was sounding like a bad interviewer of some celebrity with a complicated life. Di, who had been reticent with everyone for the last weeks, threw another stone, further out than the last, waiting for it to land with a plop in the preternaturally calm water before she answered. So many topics had become taboo.

'I don't know, but it can't be out in the open. There's Patrick and his parents. If they find out that their archenemy, me, and their so-called friend dear Steven are lovers, well, the shit would hit the fan, wouldn't it? And who'd suffer then? Patrick. They might not let Steven keep him company and they might stop him coming here. As it is, we've had a good summer out of ignorance all round.'

She tossed the stone from hand to hand. She was as brown as a nut: yes, it had been a good summer.

'As it was, when Quig informed them that the wonderful basement was undergoing further work to make it even more unrecognisable from what it once was, they calmed down. Then they were told that there was going to be an exhibition of some Porteous paintings in Kemsdown, on a theme devised by Patrick, and they liked the idea of that. They're invited to the opening of the exhibition in Kemsdown and they're keen. Steven sees that as a turning point, reconciliation, a revelation of what Patrick's like. Patrick's dying for them to go. Steven's been quite Machiavellian and devious and it's all to the good. Patrick's had free access, spent half his time here. Which was wonderful. You saw the mosaic. It took us a week. None of that would have happened if they'd known about Steven and me. Why would they ever trust him? Patrick comes first. They'll go to the preview and be proud of him, I hope. That means I can't go, of course, but it doesn't matter. I can go later.'

The seagull. Patrick's labour of love, inspired by the steps and foyers of the National Gallery. He wanted to make art you could walk over and he had created a mammoth bird that looked as if it had flung itself down at the top of the beach with one wing halfway across the path. Looking down from the path, it was still in flight, cruising down to land; from another angle it was struggling from earth. Patrick's design composed of a thousand or more carefully selected stones ranging in colour from cream to dull orange through every shade of blackish grey and the purest of white. A dozen other boys and girls had joined in and been ordered about by him. The dog walkers loved it, the dogs themselves seemed to respect it and lo and behold, more stone seagulls and a few warblings appeared on the path going through the town. Patrick had started a mosaic craze, learned to fish and grown an inch.

None of this would have happened if the love affair between Steven Cockerel and Diana Porteous had been known.

'Patrick so much wants them to go to the preview,' Di said. 'He so much wants them to be proud of it and interested in his part. But they've told him they don't want me there at the same time and I quite see their point. I couldn't do it anyway, couldn't keep up all those pretences. As for your question, is it Love? Yes, it's love of a kind. Admiration, respect, all that, but I can't ever be without reservations. I don't want anyone else, but who knows what I might think in a year's time? I'm like something just emerging from a chrysalis not yet fully formed. I've got to wait; I've got to make my own decisions and learn to do it without referring to anyone. Like I did with *our* exhibition.

Offering it to the Kemsdown, sharing it because it would achieve so much more that way. That was *my* instinct and I think it was a good instinct, all the better because it was independent and came from *my* gut. I don't want my instincts to be blurred or undermined. Steven likes control and oddly enough, so do I.'

Sarah put down her own cache of pebbles.

'Shall we ever go stealing again?' she said sadly, accepting Di's new reserve on any number of subjects. She was skating the surface.

'Look at what we've done, however haphazardly we've done it,' Di said.

'Haphazardly?' Sarah said as they walked back to the house, arms aching. 'Nothing haphazard about me and Mr Director. He's hard work. And he could still be dangerous.'

They had been right on the edge of the sea and the climb uphill was in sharp stages showing where summer storms had created steep ledges out of the shingle, making their movements more like scrambling than striding. Di stood still at the top of the slope with her hands on her hips, looking back over the calm sea as if she had created it and was pleased with her creation. Maybe her new self-assurance came from an acquaintance with happiness, but there was more to it than that. Sarah thought, *I may have to leave this story, but please, not yet. You are evading with greater ease than you ever did. You do it even better than I do. About your father, for instance.*

'Got a great idea for a new disguise,' Di said. 'There are quite a few museums and art galleries hiding their treasures like the Kemsdown. Of course we're going to do it again.'

The grand room in the schoolhouse was on a similar scale to the best room in the Kemsdown so it was an excellent bet that what looked well here would work there. The place appeared strangely denuded when they went up there with the wine. The recently removed pictures selected by Patrick were the residents of this room, leaving behind blank spaces and the ghostly marks of absence that were still a shocking novelty. There was no Madame de Belleroche to advise, no cavalier to pay court to her; it was a different space with thirty paintings, mainly portraits, gone. It was as if a whole, vital family of several generations had left the street in which they lived. The effect was appalling and liberating.

'Isn't it nice without them,' Peg said, coming in. 'I do love an empty wall.'

Peg glanced at Di. She wasn't half ice-cool, Di, Peg thought. Got a lover and her dad back, can't be bad. Di and her dad, well, well. They were polite to one another, was all; too much water under that bridge for it to move fast. Come to think of it, maybe she would only deal with her own father as long as she had a hold over him. *That makes two of us. Grace won't go near him when I'm around, but what she does when I'm not, I don't know. I think Di talks* *to her dad behind the scenes, something's up, but I'm only* *guessing. Di's like that, pretty cold,* Peg thought and then, looking at herself, *Well, it takes one to know one.* When Jones and Quig were taking the paintings out yesterday, Quig, who was usually monosyllabic, had said something silly to Madame de Belleroche and bowed to her before lifting her down off the wall. *Good morning, madam, would* *you mind coming along with me?* And Di had laughed, properly laughed.

Talking to paintings, eh? Di did it all the time. Let's face it, they were all mad as snakes. One time Quig was so bad, which he surely still is, and next you knew he's almost at home. Couldn't be the first time they'd laughed together, surely. *Maybe they're both bad. Go figure,* Peg thought. *Soon,* *I'll be out of this story, but first we've got a party to attend.*

'Do you think,' Peg said, looking at the empty wall, 'we could make it a different colour? Still don't understand why they're going. Never thought I'd see the day when you'd let any of these precious paintings out of this house, Di, still don't understand why you are.'

'I thought we'd better have a dress rehearsal somewhere else,' Di said. As explanations went it was lame and incomplete.

'Don't care, nothing to me,' Peg said. 'Main thing is we're all going to a smashing party, aren't we? Yes! So that's all right then. Never been to a first night opening of an exhibition in a *proper* gallery. Really looking forward to that. Night away as well! Can't wait!'

'Works outing for us, for the staff, bus organised,' Sarah intoned. 'There's Patrick's mum and dad, Steven and Patrick, all coming from London. We go from here, you, me, Jones. Overnight stay in a posh hotel. Champagne, dinner, bring it on! But you've got to be nice to everyone, Peg.'

'Course I will,' Peg said. 'Only I was wondering what to wear.' She was swanking across the floor, hips first.

'I'm doing bling,' Sarah said. 'And possibly feathers.'

'Patrick reckons,' Peg said, striking a pose, with one hand fluffing up her hair, 'that I should go in nothing at all. Says that's how I look best.'

'I wish you would,' Di said, looking at the empty walls and the moonlight coming in through the windows, hearing the laughter and admiring them all. Almost as much as she did the empty spaces on the walls.

Chapter Sixteen

Sticks and stones can break my bones, but words can never hurt me.

Patrick did not know why this little mantra was running through his mind like a brain worm, but the words had taken up habitation and were obscurely comforting amongst all this excitement. And it was intensely exciting, far more so than he could have imagined. He felt as proud of the paintings as if he had made them. They'd looked good in the schoolhouse: here, they looked stupendous.

The Director of the Kemsdown Museum and Art Gallery welcomes you all to this globally UNIQUE exhibition, blah, blah.

Cloake did this with ill grace, but he did it well.

The rooms were buzzing. Early evening light filtered

through rain-streaked windows. It seemed as if it had been raining all over the world for a week, scarcely easing now. Patrick was thrilled and anxious and by far the youngest person in the room which gave him a kind of distinction. The fact that the exhibition in this place that he had liked on sight was not billed as his own invention did not bother him at all. He knew it was; he was an integral part of it and that was enough. He knew it was him who had selected the paintings on loan and written descriptions and he was overwhelmingly glad it was here. He loved the way the paintings were hung, everything about it – and so many more people would see it here, including his mother and father who would never have come to see it if it had been in the cellar of Granddad's house. He'd been sad to ask Di to stay away from the preview at his father's insistence, but she'd been fine about that.

Do you mind?

No, not at all, I can go another time.

What a calm summer it had been, culminating in this. Way more thrilling than it might have been on account of being bigger and more official and it had all those other paintings he had never seen. Like that oil sketch of a blue horse, looking guilty for munching on bluebells. Then there were the paintings signed T. Hanks interspersed between the rest, each bearing the same title, *The Silent Witness*. Yes it was better that *his* exhibition should be here in this town because look at it; there were seventy people in here already and the preview had only just started and his mother and father were coming to see what he had invented. They hadn't come along together, though. It suited everyone better that he should come early with Steven to see the last of the preparation process, and they'd be along after the exhibition was officially open, ready to see the crowds and say *wow!* Dad couldn't get off work early, he said. It was all right for Steven, Dad said: he could swan off whenever he liked and his car is much posher than ours. Go with Steven, son.

The preview was everything a glamorous preview was cracked up to be. It could have been a palace. The walls were singing; everyone was looking, crowding round the paintings, peering, guessing, laughing, pointing. This was not like most previews, Steven told him. At most previews the people turned their backs to the stuff on the walls because they were too busy talking to each other and glugging the wine. That was what it was like in London, Steven said, while here, the theme forced people to look and they were looking so intently it was if they were looking for themselves. They were peering at paintings so closely they could have been looking in a mirror, searching for perfection and flaws, guessing what was behind. A game had been invented to go with the show. *Guess who did it.* Children would come in tomorrow.

Everyone was there. There was the town mayor with his chain of office, the town dignitaries and a man with a camera. There was Peg and Jones, and Sarah looking unusually discreet in a black dress and Saul looking like he'd stepped off a film set from *Downton Abbey*, all of them smartened up and Peg being shy and there was Steven hanging back, all of them alternately looking out for Patrick and then moving away to leave him to his own devices which he liked because he really wanted to be on his own. *I'll leave you to bump into bosoms*, Steven whispered to him, making Patrick giggle. Truth to tell, it had been more fun coming down with Steven alone in his great motor. That meant there was none of the constant bickering that went on between Mum and Dad in their ever-unreliable vehicles. At first, Patrick had been as happy as he had ever known himself to be.

Then, half an hour into the preview, Patrick began going outside to look for them, coming back in and scanning the crowd in case they had come in through an alternative entrance of which he was not aware. No sign of them, yet.

An hour in and Steven was trying to scale down his rage. This was part of the plan, wasn't it? To make these neglectful parents proud of their son, see what he saw, what he could do, his ideas. As far as they were concerned, the exhibition was the brainchild of the Kemsdown, using Patrick's ideas and some of his grandfather's paintings. Di Porteous was minimally involved; why should she be there at the preview? The conditions to their attendance: *No Di, or no us. We do have history, you see, Steven. Fine,* he had said. *Don't tell me, I don't need to know. She absolutely understood,* Gayle said. *Fine,* Steven said. *I scarcely know her, what's she like?* Aching with this enforced hypocrisy when he wanted to shine with love.

You bitch, Gayle, you shifty bitch. Steven had not said it and on balance he was glad Di was not here. All the pretences of him scarcely knowing her, let alone loving her, would have been as difficult to maintain as the facts he had spun to this credulous pair. He was devious, yes, but not the greatest of actors and maybe, just maybe, he had spun the plot too far. Seeing Patrick trying to be cheerful and checking the crowd made Steven go outside to phone. The night was warm and damp. As the daylight dwindled, alternative light illuminated the paintings within, creating a different and mysterious effect. The crescendo of talk ebbed and flowed. 'I don't agree,' Patrick heard someone say. 'She isn't a smuggler of drugs, how could she be? And who is this? A murderess? She looks so sweet.'

Steven felt faintly murderous himself as he went out to phone. 'Where the hell are you, Edward, old friend?'

'Just a bit of breakdown, old man, all this rain. Held up at work, you know, now waiting for the AA, be there soon.'

It was a version better to be believed than denied and Steven did not then think of the corollary to a possible deceit. He was not always good at priorities and was often prepared to accept a lie for hours before he demolished it. *Car breakdown*, he told Patrick, who nodded optimistic understanding because it had happened before; they'd be here soon, and that was enough to mollify for the moment. *Always happening*, Patrick said and went back to the paintings, examining them one by one; the ones he knew and the ones who were new acquaintances. Someone was boring on about the physicality of oil paint and the importance of semi figurative paintings in the competition for audience share.

And then, oh, look at this. One of the ones he hadn't known before but sort of recognised, showing a woman sweeping a floor, seen from behind being busy. There she was, the so-called servant he had seen with Steven in that exhibition, maybe not her but someone like her, maybe the same model with the same set to her head. Patrick's eyes followed her out of the painting and through the door beyond. She was someone he would have loved to have shown to his mother so that she could see what he saw and say, have you ever felt like that, Mum? This little painting, *Silent Witness;* she was the one he would have stolen. And it was by T. Hanks, that man in the class, Toby.

'She's going out for the day, I think,' the woman standing next to him said. 'She's done her work. She's escaping, don't you think?'

Patrick turned to face an old lady scarcely taller than himself with a lot of white hair that seemed to grow out of her head vertically. Dressed in red, she had black-lined, shining damp eyes and stood very straight, resting both hands on a cane. He had the funny thought that she and Saul could dance together like small, costumed people in a film.

'Yes,' Patrick said. 'Yes, I think she's done the work and she's going out for the day. But it's painted by someone called Toby and I don't know any girls called Toby, do you?'

He was gabbling again, saying what came into his head and it didn't matter. She was very attentive, not fidgeting like he did, moving his feet to another rhythm and using his hands to gesture. In comparison to him, she did not move at all.

'So what do you think?' the small woman said. 'Is it good, or is it good?'

'Oh yes, I like it extremely,' Patrick said, delighted to be asked his opinion, completely engaged with the conversation. 'Only it says this whole series, the Silent Witness ones, signed by TH, are painted by one bloke, this Toby. Only I just can't see these painted by a man, not that man, anyway. Just can't get it out of my head why I think it wasn't a man. Don't know why I think that, but I think it. A woman's hand, I thought.'

That sounded a bit pretentious. He stopped talking. They studied the little painting together.

'What a dear, clever young person you are,' Tabitha

Hanks said, breaking her still, upright pose to touch a lace handkerchief to her moist eyes before melting away. Patrick turned back to the picture, thinking of Peg, trying to get her to come and look, because it resembled her somehow, but then perhaps everyone looked like someone else. He turned back to the woman in red, but she was no more than a glimpse of crimson among the crowd.

An hour and a half in. No sign of his mother and father. Patrick took photos wherever he went, sent them to Di with a message. *This a very shouty party,* he said. *And I don't think my mum and dad are ever going to come at all.*

'No worries,' Steven said, coming back in. 'They've got phones off now, never been good with phones and stuff, have they? They know where we're staying, they'll be here. All this rain. Bet you're hungry.'

'I could eat a blue horse,' Patrick said and kept on looking. By this time, he was like other preview goers who looked more at the people than the paintings, only in his case with a fading hope that turned into bitter sadness.

They didn't get there, Mum and Dad, whose approval he so wanted. More people arrived in the last half-hour. The noise got louder, the laughter even louder. He could see Peg and Sarah and Jones, who looked unfamiliar in a suit. They began to gather around him. He felt hollow: before that, he felt angry, and then he was simply hungry. *Screw you, Mum and Dad. I don't need you.* He could perceive, whatever his other feelings, that this whole thing had been a massive success. If only they had been part of it. *Your loss.*

The man who gave the speeches was smiling so much that his mouth seemed to have stretched. He was being patted on the back and seemed to like it. Sarah stroked his shoulder and Patrick wondered why on earth she did that.

They spilled out into the night, reluctantly, Steven's posse and all the others who did not want to go, not just yet. They moved on to the hotel that was booked and ready, Peg, Jones, rounding them up like sheepdogs with sheep, laughing and bossing. Patrick did not quite forget his parents and decided to forget that they had forgotten him.

It was eight fifteen and a long time since he had eaten. The normal kind of hunger, as primeval as his desire for approval from his parents, took hold and predominated.

Pictures sent by Steven to Di. It's going great, but no Mum and Dad.

Think they may have other agenda. Keep doors locked.

No worries, doors locked, Di replied.

No need to tell him that this was what she intended and the doors were not locked and barred. Here she was, just like before. How many years? Fourteen since she had first come in through the metal grille at the back to steal car keys. Two years since Thomas had died and less than that since Edward and Gayle had come for their inheritance via the cellar. What had she achieved? The ability to act alone, was what. Resolve things in her own way. Be a thief and a scholar who could act on instinct.

It was significant to be alone, looking at the moody sea. The incessant rain of the week had reduced itself to a comfortable drizzle and the snuffling breeze was on a mere scale of three. It was not a dark and stormy night. All sounds were muffled and displaced; she liked that, too. In this big old schoolhouse, the installation between floors was poor despite the solidity of the building. The travelling of sound was exacerbated by Di's habit of leaving doors open and the two sets of stairs: she did not like closed doors to any of the public rooms. She would always have been able to hear someone stamp their feet or cry from the floor above. She could turn up the music as much as she liked in this grand room of hers and still at least sense the presence of someone below. It was such a rare moment to be completely alone and it felt entirely natural. This aloneness was a different state to loneliness, and was something she had never had in as many years as she could remember either after the death of beloved Thomas or before. The claustrophobia of her life in prison always haunted her. You needed aloneness to find out who you were and what you could do. There was a power in it.

Cliché. This was empty speak. To be in an empty

house with a dog seemed at the moment to be an end in itself. As happy endings went, it had a lot to recommend it.

She had thought she would use this temporary isolation to try and get back to Thomas, her Thomas, to ask him what to do; ask him if he approved of Steven and what to do next? She thought she needed to consult him, her mentor, her advisor, get some sort of wisdom from what had seemed her sole source, but that was only half the story. Really, she was waiting for something that may or may not happen.

It was a long time since she had written to Thomas. *Are you in, dear Thomas Porteous, are you in?* There was silence, as if he sent a message, saying, *No. I'm not in. You're on your own, now. But if my daughter arrives, please don't kill her.*

This is the place where I came in first to rob you of car keys. This is where I saw you sitting at this desk, with your hands bound and your wife running away to the cellar. I remember her footsteps: I heard them the moment I saw you.

This is where I sat when your daughter Gayle came in through the cellar to collect her inheritance and came up here so full of hatred she could have killed me. This is where she hit me and went back for the knife. I don't remember that nearly as much as I remember the day you and I had a party for your grandson and other children.

Where I dressed up as a witch and played games and all the children got boisterous and loved it, until it was disrupted and misinterpreted. I remember joy in this room better than I remember hatred.

And I came into this room after the party and saw you crying here, at this desk, because your daughters did not have the sense to love you and see what you were. As you did with me. So, a room of joys and sorrows and magnificence.

Tell me what to do, Thomas. What a lovely word, *shouty*. Patrick is having a shouty party and his parents have not arrived. They never intended to, did they? It was all too contrived. They engineered it knowing I would be the only one in the house, the way I so rarely am for longer than a couple of unforeseeable hours. They are not going to Kemsdown, they are coming here. And if and when they do, well. We shall talk. And this time, I shall be in control.

Are they really coming here? Or is it my imagination? Why am I so convinced that they are going to repeat what they did before? With a different motive, knowing I'm alone?

The screen was blank; the vibration from somewhere else insistent. She went downstairs. The knocking at the front door leading on to the beach grew louder as she went down. The wind was a high, blurring sound.

She could see the outline of her father's face through the panes of glass.

She let him in. *Why knock, old man, when all you have to do is push this new front door that no longer sticks and is not locked?* But then he was acting the part of a man who did not have the key to any door except his own.

'I got stones,' he said, panting. 'All I've got is stones in my pocket. They're coming, they're on their way. They phoned me to make sure you weren't anywhere else. That means they know you're alone, they're coming.'

She remembered that he had always seen the enemy coming from round the corner even when there was no enemy. That he might have shot the birds from the sky with his gun in her presence when she was small and for all that and whatever he had done, he was still the only person who had known her as a child. The one who had been there when she was born and the one who had first taught her to throw stones. And the one who had left her and come back.

'I told you, they phoned to check you were the only one home. Did it in a roundabout way, like saying was I sure you hadn't gone to Kemsdown?' He was gabbling, like Patrick did on the phone. 'I said, course she hasn't. She's probably asleep. Look, I do what you told me to do. I'm an inform-ant, aren't I? Then fucking Jones phoned. They didn't get to the Kemsdown place. They never meant to go there, they meant to come here. May already be here. Quick.'

His panic was infectious and she was not going to let it infect her.

'Come in,' she said. 'Have a drink. Thanks, Dad.'

Grace the dog growled at him although the growl was short-lived and unconvincing, her memory so selective that she could mourn the person who had once looked after her and forget the person who had tried to kill her. Grace's memory was one to admire. Forgetting was easier than forgiving.

'Your apologies have been accepted, I think,' Di said, leading the way upstairs with Grace at heel. 'She really does have an odd memory.'

'Which is more than I deserve,' Quig said. 'Have you set me up again, Di? Cool as a cucumber, you. One drink and one only, thanks.'

They sat, almost companionably, she on one side of the desk and he on the other. Quig sipped a tiny tumbler of whisky, turning it to the light and admiring the crystal of the glass as much as the liquor within. His hair was groomed and his clothes were clean. Quig brushed up well.

'Is that what you had in mind, Di? That those two would come here, find you alone and you'd do a deal with them?'

'I thought it was a distinct possibility, yes. I've got to know what they want. I wanted a chance to talk to them, on my own. If they come, that is.'

'I got plenty of stones. Never carry anything else, these days. What were you going to offer them? Tea?'

'More finding out what they want. Money; a settlement.'

'It isn't going to do, doll, it ain't going to do, 'cause it would never be enough. Come on, we talked about it. It would never do. They own the lot, as far as they're concerned. They'd rather destroy it, like terrorists with beautiful temples. And they reckon you've stolen their son. Did you seriously think they'd come in here and be magicked by paintings, like you were?'

'Money wouldn't fix it for you either?'

He admired the crystal.

'Wash your mouth out, daughter. It was never about money. Any more than it was ever about the dosh as far as you were concerned. You loved Thomas and you loved the paintings. I know it, even if I said different. I was jealous as all hell. This is about wanting to destroy what they can't have, whatever the consequences.'

'You know me better than anyone,' Di said.

'Only as far as the attitude to money goes. And yes, I'll have a little more, and yes, perhaps I do.'

They waited until gone nine o'clock. The rain fell calmly and incessantly. They were chatting, jeering a little, both sure about the keeping of distance and just a little philosophical.

'I just wanted you to know,' Quig said, 'that I didn't sell you to a bunch of thieves. You went all by yourself. So good at throwing stones. Not saying that as any kind of excuse. Only saying I didn't sell you. I went away and left you. Don't know what's worse.'

She did not respond other than nodding agreement.

'So what about this Steven?' Quig said. 'That's what I'd ask if I had a right to ask.'

'You don't have the right. We don't do conventional happy endings, do we, Dad?'

'No, girl, we don't.' And then, 'Shush,' he said. 'Listen.'

The smallest of echoes, the ghost of a presence two floors below, something that had been going on for a while and was only audible during lulls in the rain and gaps in conversation, now vibrating up the stairwell through the open door, the sense of something rather than a reality.

'Could be them,' Quig said. 'Sounds like someone using a hammer, a long way away. They've found the way in.'

'What way in?'

'The way I told you about. Where there was a door to the tunnel leading out to the beach. Bricked up one brick thick to match the rest of the wall. You know what I mean. Was the way that woman Gayle remembered, starts here, ends in one of the sheds on the other side of the road. Beautifully engineered for smugglers. My, my, they don't

284

make life easy for themselves, do they? Why tunnel in when you can walk in? You left the fucking door open.'

Quig and Di, father and daughter, went down by the back stairs to the door of the basement cellar deliberately left open from the kitchen. Stood and listened to the sound of trickling liquid.

'I did like you said,' Quig whispered. 'I left the other door unlocked. But they've got to take the hard way. Bet they brought in petrol. Or Edward did. Wait.'

They were both leaning over the elegant banister down which he had watched an angel descend. The space was dimly illuminated by the emergency lights. From their vantage point standing at the top out of sight from the bottom, Quig felt for the smallest stone in his pocket and lobbed it.

There was nothing and no one visible yet; nothing but the small sound of the pebble hitting a brick floor covered with shallow water; quite different from the sound of a stone plopping into the deep sea, a mere *splish*.

She turned on the first switch of the artful lights that lit the walls at this end of the space and illuminated the thin sheen of shining water covering the floor of the cellar. It was as if someone had turned on a tap in the middle of the floor that sloped very slightly towards the metalwork drain in the centre.

Her relief at finding the space empty was so over-powering that Di had an urge to shout and she put her hand over her mouth. Quig, intensely interested in the spectacle, shushed her. The noise made by the water was almost musical.

'Were you right about this exhibition or were you right?' he said. 'But it's only water, doll. It's not the sea, only the rain. It's the drains this time, blocked up and going mad after all this rain. That's where the water's coming from. Could be worse, doll, could be worse. Stinks, a bit though, doesn't it?'

Then from the furthest end of the room came the sound of voices.

Di turned off the light switch that illuminated their end of the room. The smell that she smelt was of earth and drains, vomit, reminding her of Grace being sick and her sluicing the floor with water into the drain. She turned on the light serving the far end. Not quite spotlit at the back of the room, among a small pile of rubble, she saw two figures, standing by a hole in the wall. Edward and Gayle, with their backs to the broken brickwork, stood by a plastic canister, totally preoccupied by arguing. The water continued to rise from the drain in the centre of the floor, almost imperceptibly drifting towards them, deeper in the middle of the room, looking like it was a river they could not cross.

Di and Quig were in relative darkness, while the two at the other end were lit. Their words were inaudible. They did not seem to notice the light because they were quarrelling so insistently, pushing each other, the one wanting to go forward, the other, Gayle, wanting to go back.

'They wanted to start a fire,' Quig whispered into Di's ear. 'That's what they wanted to do. Maybe like her mother did, twelve years ago.'

He knew that, too. He knew everything.

'They repeat themselves,' Di said. 'How can they be so stupid?'

'It isn't her. It's him.'

As they watched, the argument between the two at the far end escalated into wrestling accompanied by poisonous bickering.

'We got a choice,' Quig said. 'We can kill them, you know. We can kill them. We can knock them out with stones and let them drown like rats and bury them in the tunnel. No one would know.'

He threw another stone that landed in the gathering water with more of a splash.

'Only I never killed anything bigger than a sick dog. Can't do it. Bury them, yes, but I need them dead first. Haven't got the nerve for it, never had.'

'You and me both,' Di whispered, knowing it wasn't true. She could easily kill them.

It was like watching a show from their vantage point on the steps as the two argued, still oblivious to the light or the existence of it at all. Gayle was trying to drag him away, back out through the broken hole in the wall, pulling at him, dragging him back from the water. Edward tried to shake her off; she persisted and started to scream.

'They didn't expect the place to be empty,' Quig whispered. 'They thought there'd be stuff to burn.'

'Like the paintings they saw in the photos Patrick took. Like the junk they imagined would be here. They were planning to do exactly what Gayle's mother did all those years ago on the night I first came in.'

Di's hushed voice expressed her own wonder.

'They don't know that,' Quig said.

'Why?' she said. 'Why?'

'Don't ask why, there's no answer. He could still start a fire with that petrol he has, but she's afraid of the water. They're amateurs,' Quig said, contemptuously. 'A pair of fools. No wonder they wanted me to help.'

'They wanted you to help? You knew they wanted to do this?'

'Yes, but I never thought they would. Don't ever underestimate a fool,' Quig growled. 'And look, doll, it's not us in danger any more, it's *her.*'

Edward picked up the canister and made to walk across the floor, shaking Gayle. She grabbed him round the neck, screaming into his ear. He dropped the canister, pulled her hands away, elbowed her in the ribs. She continued to shriek and he slapped her face, hard. Gayle staggered away from him, slipped on the brick floor made lethal by the damp and fell, clumsily, into the shallow water.

You can die in an inch of water. It was less than an inch deep by the side, maybe three inches in the middle as Gayle rolled towards the drain. Di felt as if she herself was rolling towards the edge of a cliff. The sight of Gayle in the water was horrific, paralysing. *No,* she whispered. *No.*

'Bastard,' said Quig, taking a quiet aim as he threw a stone that hit Edward in the centre of his forehead, making him bellow with pain.

Di ran down the last of the stairs, splashed through the water, turned Gayle over, and dragged her back into the shallows at the bottom of the steps.

Beneath her soaked clothes she was very thin and she was shaking. She had the acetone breath of someone who starved herself. She was pitiable but Di did not feel an ounce of pity for her. She felt only the raw hatred she thought she had eradicated from her life. She had her hands round Gayle's throat and she herself shook with a weird revulsion. She made herself count to ten and loosened her grip. Gayle looked at her with dull, vacant eyes.

'I hate you,' Di hissed into Gayle's ear. 'I hate you, but I'm not going to let you die. You want to know why?'

Gayle shook her head, the slightest movement.

'Because you're Thomas's daughter and Patrick needs you.'

'Nobody needs me.' Gayle coughed out the words.

Quig stood above them both on the stairs, shouting at Edward and throwing stones, yelling, 'Get out, get out, get out, you fat bastard. Get out before I stone you to death. Get out!'

Edward stumbled away, bending through the broken aperture in the wall, ignoring the canister, not looking back for his wife.

'He left me,' Gayle said in the kitchen. She and Di were sitting alone. 'He left me.'

'He's waiting for you,' Quig said, coming back in. 'You might like to shove off before the police arrive. Off you go.'

Standing by the back door, Gayle turned the still dull eyes on Di.

'Does Patrick really need me?' she said.

'You better believe.'

Quig stood back at the top of the steps leading down into the cellar, Di next to him.

'No happy endings, girl. Not yet. Only end of another round. Good thing is, you didn't kill her.'

'No,' Di said. 'I didn't. But I could have done. It's as well to know that.'

'I know, girl, I know you could have. And she knows it, too. Better to let them destroy themselves, eh?'

'Are we really going to call the police?' Di asked, looking down and knowing the decision was hers and hers alone. She was sick of looking down; she wanted to look up.

'Break the habit of a lifetime? What do you think?'

The water on the floor of the cellar had not risen any further; neither had it receded.

'Better call the fire brigade to pump out the water, though,' Quig said. 'Can't leave it like this. It'll do damage. Don't know what Saul's going to say about his cellar.'

He sounded really worried, property-owning Quig, as if the potential for damage to the house was the most important thing of all.

Perhaps it was, Di thought.

I exist to protect people and things. That's what I do best.